Grey

Grey Tropic

Fernando Sdrigotti and Martin Dean

Dostoyevsky Wannabe Original
An Imprint of Dostoyevsky Wannabe

First Published in 2019

by Dostoyevsky Wannabe Originals

© Fernando Sdrigotti & Martin Dean

No © claims will be made against non-commercial uses of this book.
This novel is a work of fiction. The names, characters and incidents portrayed in it are the work of the author's imagination. Any resemblance to actual persons, living or dead, events or localities is entirely coincidental.

Cover design by Dostoyevsky Wannabe

dostoyevskywannabe.com

Edited by Thom Cuell

Proof-read by Sylvia Warren

ISBN-9781794357884

No parts of this publication may be reproduced, stored in a retrieval system, or transmitted in any form or by any means, electronic, mechanical, photocopying, recording, or otherwise, without the prior written permission of the copyright owner.

This book is sold subject to the condition that it shall not, by way of trade or otherwise, be lent, resold, hired out, or otherwise circulated without the publisher's prior consent in any form of binding or cover other than that in which it is published and without a similar condition including this condition being imposed on the subsequent purchaser. Under no circumstances may any part of this book be photocopied for resale.

"What shall I say about Paris? It was madness, of course, and foolery."
Fyodor Dostoyevsky, *The Gambler*

1.

There's a huge slug making its way across Gare du Nord. A black body moving towards who-knows-where. It slides, slow, oblivious to the feet that have miraculously missed it so far. Oblivious to the crushed metro tickets, the cigarette butts, the white shrivelled spots of chewing gum, the tobacco-flavoured spit and snot, the general uncleanliness of the station floor. It moves the distance of one scuffed rectangular tile and a second and half of a third. Then it's swept up by a caretaker's brush, carried along in a rapid onward drag with the rest of the rubbish and the shush of excess rainwater pushed on like a tide.

§

I get to Paris on the 5:40 a.m. train from London and it's raining. It's not far to the hotel from Gare du Nord, but it's far enough to get soaked. So I hail a cab and tell the driver where to go, in bad French. He jerks the car through traffic in a series of angry manoeuvres, as if to punish me for my linguistic inability, spraying the windows with water as we crash through puddles. Streets disappear to the sides, one after another. The city is a blurry and watery Fata Morgana. Everything feels unreal.

Grey Tropic

Henry thinks I'm arriving on Friday. That should give me one or two days to avoid calling him. Not that I don't want to see him, but I don't want to see him straight away because I need to think. Thinking needs to be done in Paris — that's the narrative protocol. Not that I even have agency over this or anything else, to be fair. Is this what I wanted for my life? Is this — to deploy even more platitudes — as good as it gets? I doubt it. I doubt being *this guy who is thinking in Paris* is as good as it gets. But here I am, once more in Paris to play the part of the confused guy travelling, looking for answers. What am I doing here? What could justify a trip to Paris these days, when at any moment I might encounter armed religious zealots running loose in the old and narrow streets, killing at random, or far right imbeciles setting tramps on fire and mobbing immigrants in the streets. When the weather is so terrible. And beyond being shot or killed by a variety of angry idiots, what other terrible things might happen to me in Paris that haven't happened to me before, or to any other guy coming to Paris for answers? Travelling is never the answer, certainly not travelling to a city that's flooding; or perhaps it is, but only in bad books or bad films. So many things that could potentially go very wrong. I get the feeling that everything is useless, that everything is boring and clichéd. This is a story that needs not be lived or told. I hate myself here. I hate whatever or whoever made this possible. "Fuck you!" I say out loud, to nobody in particular. The taxi driver abruptly stops the car and makes me walk the last five minutes, charging me two extra Euro. "Fuck you too," he says, in perfect English.

Wet and pissed off I squelch into my hotel. There's a woman behind the counter. She's not particularly happy to see me and why should she be? She wants to charge me in advance and I have no problem with that, only I don't know how long I'll stay for. I mention this to her, she understands, but she still produces a bill for the week I have reserved, saying that if I am to stay longer it can be arranged but it's hotel policy to charge in advance. I say that I've been in the hotel before, several times, many times in fact, this being my fifth or so, mostly during other failed attempts at finding answers, meaning, oblivion or some other tried and tired objective, and that this is the first time I've been asked to pay in advance. I explain all this in those exact words, well aware that they'll be of little interest to her, because they're self-indulgent horseshit, and they're scarcely of interest even to me. She stares back blankly, doing something with her mouth, opening the inside of it while the front stays closed, like a snake drawing yolk from a swallowed egg. Is this some kind of nonverbal 'fuck you'? I don't even know why I bring this money thing up. I don't care really, as money isn't an issue, not here, not at all. If she asked me to pay for a month in advance I'd probably pay anyway and to be fair I just want to get to my room and have a lie down. I tell her that I don't care, that money isn't an issue — money is never an issue, really, I add, like a total cunt, and I throw some money on the counter, the exact money, knowing that if I put my hand in my pocket it would close around banknotes. Adding nothing, she hands me the keys and points down the stairs, towards room 29. I know where it is, I say with a sense of ownership, and leave. I can hear her cursing me under her breath.

The room looks as I remember it. I can see traces of myself at different moments in time, as though this three-dimensional space were a sort of second body, spattered with material evidence of all my failures, unfinished stories, disappointed women, ideas jotted down on notebooks that were never followed through, and some other parts that apparently are anchored in real life, in someone's life, perhaps mine, but one that has escaped me, gone on alone without me. A vast but extremely faded stain on the carpet beside the bed — a footnote of some kind. Memories of bellowing in drunken anguish float up from somewhere. A mild headboard shaped dent in the wall — another footnote.

Images mix in my head: did this happen in my first trip, did it happen in the second, are these recollections from someone else's life? Am I remembering someone else's memories? What the fuck is going on? What is real here? What is autobiography and what belongs somewhere — to someone — else? Is there a difference between biography and fiction? Aren't all biographies lies and all fictions factual documents? What have I imagined and what have others imagined? What am I thinking? What does it mean? Since when do I think like this? It makes no sense.

I arrange my things and lie down in bed. I wake up four or five hours later, with the TV on. A woman is saying something in French. What, I don't know. I don't really care. If it added anything to my limited life — to this fantasy where I find myself — I'd very likely be able to speak French. But for my isolation to be complete, French can't be part of this story. I will spend the rest of the day watching television, confused, and alone. It has to be this way.

§

By six or seven p.m. I can't take it anymore and call Henry. I thought I could stretch it longer but it's impossible. To be fair, the idea of staying alone and doing fuck all in my room was pretty infantile to begin with but I'm pretty sure the thing I witnessed left me with no choice but reaching out to someone, something, familiar. And the only thing familiar here is Henry. OK, other things might have been lost, or haven't been introduced yet, as the idea of things being familiar or not is always in a state of crisis. And maybe some other familiar space exists under the surface of all this but how could I know it? But Henry. It came down to Henry.

A couple of hours ago I went to the window. It was raining, as it will rain for the rest of this story. I couldn't see much through the glass, nothing across the back garden save for a small area under one of the trees, on the left. There are three windows to that side, one for each floor. The top two of them were closed, the bottom one partially opened. It was very noisy with the rain cutting across the leaves. And dark, almost night dark. I focused my eyes on a tiny gap in the curtain on this bottom window and in that sliver of space between the curtains I could see clearly into the room beyond: a bit of wall, a bit of bed, and a dick. The rest of the body was out of sight apart from a hand which was tugging — tugging, actually pulling and releasing then pulling again, like someone twanging an elastic rope, not like actual wanking — a dick.

A dick.

I closed my curtains and sat on my bed still, trying to understand what I had just seen, and how could it relate to the rest, to the whole — these sorts of things wouldn't happen whimsically and there must be some logic behind me seeing a man pull his dick like a rubber eel in a room across a garden. For a moment the wind caught the rain and made it undulate against the glass of my window, and I suddenly had the impression that the space around me, the room, the walls, the night, and the city beyond was being tugged and released, the walls of the room stretching and relaxing like The Great Rubber Dick of Reality in the hands of an uncaring God looking for Strange Thrills in a Shitty Parisian Hotel Room in the Rain. Everything has a logic. Everything is a logically-ordered narrative that brings all things together. Everything must have one. Or maybe there isn't a logic. I feared for this terrible possibility and it felt too harrowing to be considered. But more importantly, the thought of someone tugging at his dick in a lonely hotel room in Paris, and me witnessing it just by chance, filled me with sadness. What need there was for that? And so I called Henry.

The phone call was short. In under a minute I managed to communicate that: A) it's raining like in

The Flood; B) for some reason I don't have an umbrella — and I should have an umbrella; C) therefore I can't leave the hotel until it either stops or Henry brings me something to keep the water away from me — all pretty simple. In this same minute Henry tried to retort to my proposal saying that I could borrow "*un parapluie de l'hotel*" or just take one from the lobby, as is the "*coutume ces jours-ci à Paris*." To this I just replied "Henry, don't be stupid, and speak English" and so it was arranged that I would meet him half an hour later.

§

I walk up to reception: the place is empty save for a guy behind the counter. I walk towards the door without greeting him and lean against the frame. God it's raining. I don't think I've ever seen rain like this. Not in Paris to be sure. Maybe in Vietnam or India. This is most unusual. But there's also something peaceful about this rain, not only because the streets seem to be empty, but because sounds seem to be muffled behind the water. I can't hear any cars, or sirens. No people, no explosions, no sounds of shotguns or suicide vests or skinheads assaulting refugees.

I walk back towards the lobby and as soon as I step with my right foot I hear a cracking sound underneath.

I look down and realise I've crushed a snail into a sticky brown slurry with broken shell fragments. While I'm looking down I hear Henry calling my name. I turn around and there he is, covering himself under a huge green umbrella with the words Alliance and Leicester in white, half a metre or so away from me. He's carrying another umbrella in his other hand that looks exactly the same (unopened), same colours. We shake hands — he's got a limp handshake and I guess I do too — it's better than trying to crush everyone like a total cunt. He passes me the umbrella and I put it up and we start walking, but the umbrellas are so large that we're a good five feet apart as we walk side by side. Henry shouts something under our green rainforest-like canopy, but with the rain on the canvas roof and the rush of it all around us I can't make it out. "What?" I shout back. He smiles and shakes his head, looking down at his feet. This pisses me off, for some reason I can necessarily understand. "Wanker," I call him. "What?" He shouts back. I smile at him and keep walking. "Did you need to bring Alliance and Leicester umbrellas?" I shout. "I can't hear you," Henry shouts back. "Oh, fuck off," I say and I feel better. Everybody feels better after insulting Henry — it's his super power.

Two minutes later we're seating at a table at Au Pied

du Sacré-Cœur, this little family restaurant just a few steps down from the hotel door, a picturesque location and exactly the kind of setting where two characters like Henry and I would be tempted to sit down to eat. The place is empty save for us. We order fast and start drinking fast too — a bottle of house red because although I can afford a better wine Henry wouldn't deserve anything better. We have made up our minds to drink plenty tonight and Henry has made his mind up that I will be fronting the bill. It's always been the same.

"I'm happy you are here, bro," says Henry with a bit of a French accent, perhaps thinking about the wine.

"Me too," I say. "But I wasn't going to call you until tomorrow or after tomorrow."

"Why did you call, then?"

"I saw this guy, across the garden, tugging at his dick."

"Uh?"

"Yes, he was tugging at his dick. I opened the window and there was the dick, across the garden, being tugged behind a curtain of rain — it was incredibly sad."

"Tugging, like wanking?"

"I can't tell. It seemed he was tugging and pulling at it…"

"Wanking."

"No man, that's not how people wank."

"People wank all kinds of ways."

"Do you pull your dick like that when you wank? Of course you do."

"No, I'm not saying that I do, but you know... Anyway. Sounds strange."

I start to say something but have a drink from my wine instead, wondering why I brought this strange thing up at all. The wine tastes harsh and acidic, like it's come from a bottle left open all night. "It's good to be back" I say, in an attempt to feel like it's good to be back and not really aware whether it is good to be back or not and still none the wiser as to why I'm back. But the fact is that I'm back.

§

Two hours later we're yelling and pissing. I'm pissing in wild circles toward a urinal, the part of my mind in control right now thinks it's taking part in some kind of piss rodeo. We've stormed into the steamed up bowels of a grisly bar draped in drunken thirty something characters like us, threaded through with twenty somethings that we're trying to fuck. We're somewhere down Rue des Abessess but there are no tourists, suspiciously. It could be a Latin place, judging by the music, but it could as well be anywhere and anything or it could be all a product of my imagination. "It could as well be anywhere," I feel like shouting and I do, showing a proficient connection between my drunken thoughts and my mouth, one that somehow bypasses my brain. Henry is laughing, manically, also taking part in some kind of whirlwind attack on the urinal — he doesn't hear me. It's all pretty disgusting. But as a visitor in Paris, I need to do something to offset the city's all pervading sense of superiority over me. Can I win against it? Can I beat the axis of power, money, empire, literature, film? Can I find a niche, a burrow in the city from which to fight back, destroy it, destroy its aura? Very likely not — I'm thinking nonsense.

Soon we stumble back into the bar. There is a demure, bespectacled young woman there whose hand I take and, leading her away from the bar, I playfully begin mock-dancing with her. She seems to be enjoying it and dances with me. We whirl in a semi blur — I stumble amiably and she reaches an arm around me to steady me. We dance and dance and a sense of real achievement begins to flood through me. Now Paris feels like Paris in old stories about Paris: Paris in the 30s, Paris of the 60s. It's all here, crowded into this bar — Latin jazz, couples dancing. There's

Hemingway over there, steering a drunken Scott Fitzgerald towards the door. There's a bunch of *engagé* students smoking, looking at their watches, waving books at each other, planning intelligent revolutions and middle class excursions into the night, and experimental novellas, oblivious to the refugee crisis and the wars in the Middle East and the USA nuking North Korea any time soon and all the rest of the shit that's going on. La Maga and el Negro Olivera could be here, Rocamadour trusted to a nanny hired through an agency, paid for — reluctantly — by the French state. Everyone is here — it feels as if I had arrived. I put my hands on the girl's arse and she grinds her pelvis into mine, I can hear champagne being opened on the bar behind me, laughter and cheers. Just then Henry stumbles over and puts his arms round us both, doing a double-take at the girl. "I got some coke. Let's do coke." As if Henry was now the Pied Piper, we follow him to the toilet.

There we pile into a cubicle and rack up some lines. The girl seems very keen to get high, and each of us in turn bends over the toilet seat and snorts a line. And another. After each line she holds out her hands like a mime and says "… *ah… oui… ah… oui…*" It's hilarious, this coked-up Marcel Marceau moment, something that adds a great humorous touch, albeit one somehow to be expected, being where we are. And then we head back out to the bar and get some whiskies, bouncing and urgent, sniffing, stabbing through the space to the bar with definite, ad-campaign movements, feeling powerful like the reasons the bar and the night and the city existed, but to everyone else looking like abominable wankers of the worst kind. Then other people in the bar are edging away from us in disgust and then, just like that, we're walking in the street once more.

I try to talk to Henry but he can't hear me and soon I forget what I wanted to say and it doesn't matter anymore. We are zigzagging under the rain, under two umbrellas we stole from the bar lobby. And it's roads and roads; crooked unpronounceable roads; sites of who knows how many atrocities, how much or how little history. Some flights of stairs up and others down. Until we end up at this place called Au Rendez Vous des Amis, right on the top of Montmartre, just as my mood begins to swing to unhinged ennui. We go straight into the toilet and do some more coke and then hit the bar and have a couple of beers with some tramps. We're talking and suddenly I realise we're talking in English and that I quite enjoy the conversation although it's not come around to me or the pointlessness of this night. Nice tramps — stinky but charming. Henry keeps talking about politics, about Le Pen and ISIS and multiculturalism, things the tramps might find interesting, while I concentrate on taking in the place, enjoying the fact that I'm here talking to people I've never met before about things I don't really care about but that at least this isn't the typical Parisian night and I'm not a cliché. Or maybe not that much of one.

And then a jump cut in my mind and it's another bar, this corner place in the streets below Sacré-Cœur. My drunken consciousness succeeds in fixing its name in memory: Au Clair de Lune. I suspect this is a residual memory from another time or another life, because I don't even remember how we got here and tomorrow I will forget it all anyway. But now we're sitting at a table on the terrace and we're still drinking heavily and we still have some coke left. Henry is going on and on about the possibilities of this meta-fictional way of writing to this French couple. I miss half of what he says but I can tell it's a load of bullshit anyway because Henry wouldn't be able to write a shopping list, let alone anything intelligent. And what the fuck does he mean by meta-fictional? He must be high — he's invincible and irritating. I ask Henry for the coke and rush to the toilet once more. It's running out. I snort what's left. And then at some point in the night the lights go out.

§

Then it's the morning after. Or something like a morning. But more like some viscous secretion of time, in which the night before and the morning after blend into the same amorphous blob. It's not the morning after but it's certainly not the night before. It's something in between. I don't really know what it is. It's just opening my eyes and confusedly scanning around the room to learn that I'm no longer in the bar, that there is light coming through the curtains, that it smells like sick and that the vomit is on my side of the bed, all over my shoes. I hate these jump cuts. In cinema and in literature and particularly in life.

I sit on the bed. I get dizzy, feel nauseous, run to the toilet. The lights are on, it smells like piss and vomit; in a matter of seconds I throw up in the sink for I wouldn't dare to stick my face within one meter of that toilet seat. I throw up with ease and I can't really tell what I was drinking from it but I get hints. I remember drinking red wine, but there's something with a sweet aniseed taste coming from my mouth and I can't tell what it is. I throw up and throw up and it's raining and the toilet window was left open and there's mud on the floor, a mix of dirt and fuck knows what, that makes vomiting even sadder. I finish puking and rush back to the room and sit on the bed. (I never looked at my face in the mirror. This will be important: I never looked at my face in the mirror after vomiting.)

And I just sit there, looking around, lost and increasingly sad. I don't like the turn things have taken. And if it weren't raining I would go out and walk around for hours, cry under some bridge, or just sit alone in some square, or just jump into the Seine and die. But it's raining and I can't see the umbrella anywhere in the room and I have this flashback of a Scouse guy arguing with me over the umbrella, just round the corner, accusing me of stealing two Alliance and Leicester umbrellas down Passy earlier in the day, and me trying to explain that it couldn't have been me, that I don't even know where Passy is. I think he was wearing an Alliance and Leicester t-shirt. I'm sure he was a short, ginger type, and that I found him utterly despicable. I don't remember how the situation was resolved and whether he took the umbrella or I just lost it. Another black spot in an already giant black hole. And here the telephone starts ringing. It can only be Henry or somebody calling a wrong number, so I don't bother answering. The phone rings for what seems an hour and then it stops.

I know for certain that the phone will start ringing again and sure it does. I could answer and get things done once and for all but I feel a certain pleasure in making Henry wait. But then, as the telephone is still ringing there's a knock at the door. I'm half naked — I won't answer. There's another knock. And a louder knock. And then it feels like they could knock the door down. I must act: I roll across the bed and stumble towards the door. I get my foot caught in something — perhaps my clothes — and nearly fall down on the way. I open the door; the telephone stops ringing at the same time.

"Hello!" says the man standing outside. He's wearing a pair of swimming shorts, brown leather sandals and long white socks underneath. That's all. He has a huge moustache, like a Victorian strongman. His chest is incredibly hairy.

"Hello!" I say, trying to pretend I'm not surprised by this unwanted intrusion, by the new character joining this farce.

"Can I come in?" he says briskly in a thick French accent as he pushes towards me and into my room, "I must see something." I have no clue why he's speaking in English instead of French. But he does speak with an accent, at least there's that.

Brisk, brisk, everything about him is jumpy. He walks right in while I stand perplexed holding the door handle. I'm still all caught up in booze and charlie from the night before and I don't know if I'm awake or still dreaming or how much time has actually gone past since I arrived. Has some latent gay part of my unconscious assumed control? That at least could be interesting, an unexpected departure.

He walks up to the window and looks out of it, then turns his head and looks at me, about to say something. Then he pauses, and smiles. I realise that he's looking at me, stood here in just my boxer shorts. It feels less like a dream, suddenly.

"I need to look at the outside of my room!" he brays. I'm not sure what to say.

"OK," I say.

He puts one foot up on a stool to adjust his sock, and as he does his swimming shorts flap open, giving me a big flash of hairy balls and cock. I look away quickly. He realises that I've seen his balls and cock and smirks. But quickly he starts peering out of my window: he opens it so he can look out through the rain.

"My room is there, look!" He tells me, beckoning me to come over. I stand next to him, as far as I can next to him. He points across the garden, and I see which room he is pointing to: he's pointing to the dick twanger's room. Suddenly I feel even more uncomfortable. Just as I realise this, I feel his hand idly caress the small of my back.

"Something keeps making my room smell!" He says, incensed.

"Smell?" I say, moving away from his hand and looking for some clothes. I find my shirt. I start putting it on.

"I think there's a bird's nest, or dead pigeon, bats, or something in the gutter by my window!" he says excitedly, his right hand pulling the fabric of his shorts.

"Well," I say. "Can you see anything?"

"No!"

"Well. You can ask at reception they might be able to help."

"THEY DO NOTHING!" he screams, very high-pitched now. He's all flustered. Nervous. Maybe even sweating.

There's a silence. He looks down.

"I must go," he says quietly, embarrassed by his outburst. I watch as he walks towards the door, looking at me as he walks out, and closes the door behind him. Just before it's fully closed, he opens it again. "I'm Stephan!" he says cheerfully and leaves.

He was a digression, a strange digression, I guess. He wasn't necessary. But he had to come. And he made the best of his moment in the spotlight, leaving me confused and forlorn. Was he necessary? Things could be even worse.

I close the door. I go back to bed. I fall asleep. I wake up round midday.

§

And then I'm walking under the rain, covering myself with a Canal+ umbrella I stole from the reception. My Doc Martens start to give up on me; they make a squeaking sound with every step I take — it's unnerving. I must be only 50 metres away from the hotel but I decide it's a good moment to walk into a tiny café on Rue Caulaincourt, Café de la Butte, because walking in this weather, however picturesque and good for the story, is incredibly stupid.

When I cross the door all faces look my way, the three of them: two old guys and the old lady behind the bar. They don't smile but they don't frown either — instead they come across as curious to see someone walking in at this time, in this weather, in this day and age. The walls are covered in old photographs and strange tiny flags that I can't place — they belong to some ancient sport, perhaps long forgotten, their heraldry and colours now fading. I spot a black and white photograph in one corner of a good looking girl of about twenty; she's dressed in cycling gear and has a huge smile; the name "BABETTE" is written in one corner, with a sharpie, in large capital letters. It dawns on me that the little flags must be cycling trophies or something like that. Almost at the same moment I realise that Babette is actually the old lady behind the bar she asks me what I want and I order a coffee. Just that, a coffee, "*un café, s'il vous plaît.*"

I go back to stare at the walls and I bump into a TV set. A morning show, with a guy and a woman with sexy, shiny, shaved legs talking about who knows what. They seem to be having a good time, laughing and poking one another, whilst they speak their incoherent language fast, very fast, and the people in the TV studio clap their hands and go "ooooooohhhhhhh". Suddenly a giant Sumo wrestler — the proper stuff, wearing nappies and obese and carrying a geisha, a French girl disguised as one — walks into the scene and the set explodes with laughter and excitement. I can't follow what goes on but the presenters seem surprised by the Sumo wrestler turning up like that, unannounced and carrying a geisha, or at least they pretend to be surprised. I really don't know what to make of this. And suddenly the sumo wrestler walks out of the screen, while the audience claps and launch into a combination of "oooooooohhhhhhhs," "aaaaaaaaahhhhhhhs" and "eeeeeeeehhhhhhhs". "Racists" I say to myself, by way of an explanation.

Babette brings the coffee to my table; she smiles but she doesn't speak to me and I'm thankful she doesn't. I stay for some moments mesmerised by the coffee, the way the vapours climb into the air, disappear two or three centimetres away from the cup. Just as I'm about to make my mind up that I need to pack my stuff and jump on the next train back to London I see Henry's name vibrating on my mobile phone — of course I won't answer. The telephone rings for quite a while — the people in the café stare at me. The situation becomes too uncomfortable. I finally answer.

"What?"

"Hey!" he says. He sounds happy.

"What's up?"

"What you up to?"

"I'm having a coffee round the corner from the hotel. An old man harassed me earlier — I think he was the penis twanger."

"No way!"

"Yes, man. He came to my room, grinning and flashing his balls."

"You're telling me something very strange."

"It happened — it was nasty."

"Awful."

"Yes."

"What did he want?"

"I don't have a clue?"

"How do you know it was him?"

"A gut feeling."

"Interesting…" he says. "I don't see the connection between him and…"

"Me neither."

"He could be a digression."

"I think we've already given him too much importance for him to be just that."

"Anyway… Don't worry… What you up to later?"

"Nothing. I'll go back to London?"

"No way!"

"Yes way!"

"Listen, buddy. I know you're going through some kind of unspeakable personal crisis, that there's a lot under the surface of the iceberg of yourself, but don't go back — things will make sense. There are things that are clear from the start. Other times sense is born in the process. I'm sure things will turn out OK. BELIEVE. And you're already here." I have no idea of what he means — he must still be drunk.

"What the fuck are you on about, Henry?"

"Meet me at 4 p.m. outside Bellville metro station."

"What for?"

"It's a surprise."

"I don't like surprises," I say.

"I know. Meet me there! You need a surprise. I can only promise it'll be a pleasant surprise," he says and hangs up. This is so un-Henry. As if he had gone through the kind of transformation that in a bildungsroman is generally reserved for the main character, in this case myself. But this is not a bildungsroman. And, am I the main character of this? What if I'm fooling myself and not only am I in a story that lacks direction, but in one where I'm not even the main character? What if the point of this story is to narrate the delusion of a character who insisted on seeing himself as the main character but is actually some minor occurrence in an overarching grand narrative? What if Stephan the dick twanger is the main character? What if all the characters in this story share a certain dramatic hierarchy? What if this is some kind of statement? God, don't let this be a statement.

I go back to the coffee and it's no longer steaming. It must be cold now, all because of Henry and his fucking surprise. Everyone is staring at me even more than just a while back, all because of this stupid conversation in English. I imagine that I should probably do something very spontaneous and ask aloud whether I should stay or go. I don't do it in order to exacerbate everyone's discomfort, even my own. So instead I look around, slightly confused and still indecisive. What to do? What to do?

I spot a crumbled copy of *Le monde* on the table next to mine. I lean in and get it and start passing page after page of letters, words, paragraphs that I can't read. I look at the pictures instead. Le Pen, Macron, some other politicians (I guess), an impoverished black person somewhere in the impoverished black world, pictures of rubble — probably somewhere in Syria — ISIS wankers pointing their fingers to the sky, pictures of this Juncker guy and Theresa May, holding hands, and then I get to the weather page. There's a five days weather forecast special and it's all clouds and drops, all rain. There are images of flooding rivers, of bridges with their arches almost fully submerged underwater, the Zouave with the water up to his neck, people grabbing their heads, that kind of stuff. I recall having seen images of flooded Paris before, in some book, or on the internet. Or maybe I just dreamed about them. Maybe it never happened. Can Paris really flood? Could Paris disappear under water like Atlantis? Right now it certainly feels like it could — it feels like the end of time.

When I leave the bar it's still raining.

PARIS — Rue Jacob

2.

A huge slug stuck to the window of the train carriage, on the outside, leaving a slimy mark while it motions slowly on the way up. A kid is watching it from the inside, nose squashed against the window, forehead too, leaving a greasy mark on the glass, and a dialogue between two shiny marks is like this established. And soon light of day, rain, and soon darkness: a tunnel. Then more daylight and more rain. Grey and beige buildings, they all look the same. And colourful neon signs.

The rain washes the slug away and the kid stays against the glass, watching the city scroll behind the drops, behind the slime, and the grease from his own face.

§

I bump into Henry just outside Belleville's Metro. He was already there when I arrive. He has a large blue umbrella with white dots — there's something written on it but I can't read it. I find his umbrella funny. He laughs at my transparent umbrella, or about the "Victoria's Secret" written on it. We don't shake hands or say anything. He starts walking and I follow him. After more or less two or three blocks under the rain it occurs to me that I don't know where we're heading.

"Where are we going?" I shout.

"Neva's," he shouts back and I feel that's all the information I need to know. I mean, I should probably ask who Neva is, but I feel Henry is being cryptic so that I will ask him who Neva is so that he can play mysterious so that he can feel a bit better about himself, somehow more in control, less pathetic, powerless and useless. So I just keep on walking, confident that in due time I'll find out what's going on, what this is about, who this Neva is. But more importantly, confident that it won't really matter, that soon I'll be boarding the Eurostar back to London.

Soon we stop in front of a large wooden door. Henry keys in a code — 6831, I see his right index finger hammer the keys — and we walk into the building. There's a narrow wooden set of stairs to the right and some doors to the left, a garden towards the back of the building, a round fountain in the garden, rain. We shut our umbrellas — Henry's is a Credit Suisse one, I find out then and there — and place them against the wall by the doors, where I count at least ten umbrellas of different colours, sizes, and makes, from all sorts of brands. We take the stairs and climb, one, two, three, four, five floors over creaking wet wood, surprisingly quickly and without complaints. Then we walk towards a door with a huge sticker on it — I think it's Yukio Mishima with a sword — and Henry opens the door and we walk in without announcing ourselves. It smells like weed and fried onion.

"*Bonjour*," says a female voice.

"Hi," says Henry. I nod with my head, a pointless act, for Neva — it is Neva, as I'll soon learn — is with her back towards us, watching a laptop screen closely. Then she turns around — I can't see her features very well due to the smoke but she looks around thirty, with large eyes, and a thin face.

"Capricorn!" she says and turns around back again.

"What?" says Henry.

"He's a Capricorn," she says and coughs. "Aren't you a Capricorn?" she asks me.

"Ariel, nice to meet you," I say.

"Are you a Capricorn, or not?" asks Henry.

"Yes, I'm a Capricorn, I guess," I say.

Neva smiles. She turns around back towards the screen.

"I knew it. Have a seat," she says and I look around and I can't see a sofa or chairs or anything to sit on, save for some round cushions. They are arranged around a low coffee table, and I see Henry motioning towards them, so I do the same and soon we're sitting over there, where it smells like cat piss, watching the world from a strange angle, me thinking that there aren't any other signs of cats, so it could very well be human piss. "I sensed your energy, Capricorn," says Neva turning around. "I sensed it for a while. You got off at Goncourt, am I right?"

"No, I got off at Belleville," I say.

"Strange," she says. "I sensed your energy at Goncourt. It must be the rain." Henry takes his index finger to his right temple and knocks a few times and winks — I find this minimal act of betrayal appalling and telling of his weakness, his constant need to seek for reassurance. "Do you guys want to smoke? I'll finish with this in a minute," she says.

"I'm fine," says Henry.

"I'll pass," I say.

"As you wish," she says.

"What you working on?" asks Henry. There's a long silence. "What you working on, Neva?" he asks again.

"Editing a very very very drafty chapter," she answers.

"Neva is a writer," says Henry rather seriously, now reeling back from his suggestion that Neva might be crazy.

"Oh, yeah? What do you write?" I ask, as it's mandatory to feign interest in the things so-called writers waste their time on. She turns around once more. Yes, big eyes, rather pretty, a bit wasted, mid 30s or younger.

"What do you mean what do I write?" she asks. There's something tense in her voice.

"Yes. Fiction? You know…"

"Everything is fiction…" she answers.

"I guess so," I say. "Sorry for asking." This conversation is going nowhere.

"But I'm working on a historical novel about the Paris Commune," she says.

"She's a journalist," says Henry.

"I thought she was a writer," I say.

"I sense your pain, Capricorn," she says and I don't know what to answer.

"I don't know what to say to that," I say.

"Don't say anything," says Neva.

"Yes, mate, don't say anything," says Henry with a huge grin on his face.

"Why don't you roll yourself a joint? Go on," says Neva and without waiting for my reply throws a large metallic box towards me. I catch it before it hits me in the head.

"OK," I say. I open the box on the table and search inside it. Lost in the tobacco there's a huge rock of hashish, the size of a golf ball. "I hope you didn't carry this in your arse," I say. Neva finds this very funny, she laughs. Henry pretends to laugh.

"Not sure how that got here; but not in me," she

says. I surprise myself finding that part of her retort — "not in me" — rather enticing but I try not to make too much out of it. Instead I put some tobacco to the side and scan around for a lighter, to melt a bit of hash. Perhaps after reading my mind once more Neva throws the lighter in my direction and it falls on the floor by my side.

"What's cooking?" asks Henry.

"I was cooking pasta... But I burnt the sauce," she says. "When I'm writing I forget the world."

"It can happen," says Henry. "I have lost track of time, writing poems, a story, or just jotting down some ideas on paper." I didn't know Henry fancied himself a writer too but I'm too busy melting the hashish to say anything. And there are more urgent matters than Henry's fancies. Who's this Neva? What's that accent? I can't tell where her accent's from. Sounds continental, but she's not French, I can tell that. There's no trace of the typical French sound, *ze* pasta, *ze* hashish, *ze* Capricorn, etc. And if she were French Henry would be speaking in French, just to write me out and score points against me.

"If you want we can go out and bring a pizza... Or some cheese and bread, and a nice bottle of red," says Henry.

"Yes," I say. I have already piled up a large amount of

hashish, about the circumference of a two Euro coin, one centimetre tall.

"Ana is on her way with food," says Neva, "That's a lot!" she adds pointing towards my artwork with her head. I don't listen and proceed to roll. Ana must be another one, another nutter.

"Ana is her flatmate," says Henry.

"Oh, I see," I reply. I look around: it's a tiny studio flat. The room must be four by four. The cushions are around the short coffee table, by the wall. On the opposite wall is the desk. By the main door there's a bunk bed. And then the door that leads to the kitchenette. No sign of a toilet, but there must be one, somewhere. Only now I realise how small the flat is. At least they have a window. I ignore how someone, let alone two someones, can live in such a small space, but here we are. "Where you guys from?" I ask, perhaps in order to come to some xenophobic conclusion about how people from x or y live.

"Oh, lots of different places," says Neva and pops up from her chair and motions towards the main door and then leaves.

"Oh, well," I say and I finish rolling my joint. Henry is acting all cocky. He wants me to ask him who the fuck this Neva is, where does he know her from. I won't give in to this either. Instead I put the joint in my mouth, feeling a warm pride at its weight between my lips.

"Holy shit!" Henry shouts. "What the hell is that?"

"This is a joint Henry. I know you know that."

"That is a big joint, man."

"Yes, it is."

Henry's one of those guys who can't get enough weed, but has always had too much weed. He'll always be the first to inquire about it, but when it finally reaches him it's too much and he falls slumped in the corner for hours like someone's old coat. As a result, whenever weed appears he always begins a little nervous and fascinated conversation about it and everything takes on a sudden teenage turn — smoking with Henry feels like what bringing a porn mag to school used to feel like. I light up the joint — the hashish tastes sweet and strong.

Soon Neva reappears with Ana, who rolls in on a pair of rollerblades, carrying a shopping bag with some kind of food inside. She doesn't really try to stop and runs into Henry — she grabs his shoulders to break a fall and then hangs onto the wall. "Yeah!" She says triumphant, staring at us.

"Hi Ana," says Henry, "Still wearing those skates?"

"Hi Henry," says Ana, extending one hand towards his face, fingers outstretched like a wizard. "Still wearing those SHOOOES?" She says "shoes" as if time has slowed down. As she says it she slowly lowers her rigid outstretched arm and extends one long finger to point at Henry's brown brogues, as if casting a spell on them to magically turn them into something stylish. I'm quite sure this is really happening, that the shoes will turn into a nice new pair of Italian shoes, although it's at this point I realise that this isn't because things tonight will take on a fantastical turn but because I've become overwhelmingly high, very fast. To me it seems like some ancient conversation is occurring between two profoundly necessary parts of reality's subtle weave — Anubis is greeting Osiris. Or even: two different drafts have overlapped and my existence is now a palimpsest.

"Yep, still wearing shoes," Henry retorts, artlessly.

I smile, red-eyed, glad the important greeting ritual has been completed. Memories or fantasies of memories come back to me. And I recall Henry and Ana, Ana and Henry, in other places, other times, greeting one another just like this. We've been together for a while, I think. We might not remember but we are old friends and I'm off my fucking head. Ana pushes herself off the wall towards a round cushion and slumps down. Neva has come back with a pint glass of water. I pass the joint to her, and she looks at it.

"Holy shit," she says, lighting it again. She puffs out a large smoke ring towards the ceiling — it hangs in the air over us like a grey halo.

Half an hour later I've begun to realise that the room is actually a fantasy — a fantasy within a fantasy — that's being projected onto a two dimensional surface that surrounds me like a curtain in a hospital ward. It's disconcerting, but it's making me laugh. Henry is slumped in the corner, Ana sat to his side. She seems to be having an intense conversation with him, though Henry is quite clearly asleep. She keeps showing me her knickers, I think intentionally. They're blue and very big and the insides of her legs are white and bony and fleshy and they are driving me insane. Rain falls against the windows and I enjoy the sensation of sitting inside this soothing rushing sound. The more I think of it, the more it starts to feel like the top of my head is rushing with it, rushing upwards, and the rest of my body rushing downwards into the earth and Ana's knickers. Neva is in a meditative posture, eyes closed, breathing deeply.

Suddenly Neva starts saying *Om* quite loudly, a long continuous *Om*. She opens her eyes and looks at me and says *Om* more meaningfully, nodding with her head, encouraging me to join in with this thing. Ana is already saying *Om*. Neva is still looking at me so I start saying *Om* too. Henry is slumped in the corner. We sit there, the three of us, saying *Om*, until I stop to smoke a bit more of the joint. I feel blissful. However contrived, all of us saying *Om* has left a peaceful flavour in the air. The rain all around us and these two women who seem fragrant. For some moments I forget about all my worries and anxieties and I just sit, as if nothing else had ever existed.

"You know what…" Ana is speaking absentmindedly and rubbing her thighs together, moving her skates backwards and forwards across the floor.

"We know what," Neva says proudly, smiling. It doesn't make any sense, nothing does, but to make things even more incoherent I suddenly imagine Neva's proud torso as the brightly painted figurehead on an old ship, forging through the waves. "The I-Ching tells us all," she goes on, and reaching behind her, she pulls out a heavy book in a purple velvet bag. "The I-Ching told me about you, Capricorn," she says, pointing at me with her big eyes.

"It's Ariel," I say, stupidly, and then giggle. Neva gives me a stern look.

"The… I…Ching…" Ana says, slowly, with reverence, like it's an Indiana Jones movie and soon a beam of sunlight will shine through the window illuminating Neva's beaten-up paperback I-Ching, and it alone. But it doesn't happen outside of my imagination, half of which embarks on a quest with Ana, to bring the holy I-Ching back to the Dalai Lama, who rejects us with violence and effusive swearing for bringing him a Chinese oracle. I snap back to reality. Looking for the meaning. The meaning is somewhere in Ana's mind, just not available to me, I decide.

Neva starts trying to describe my character with the help of the ancient Chinese oracle, reading from a random hexagram, and I happily nod and agree with all of her appraisals, content with the attention, however wrong or nonsensical, until she's left looking satisfied and slightly horny.

"I knew it," she says. I nod meekly, un-amazed by the miracle in which someone read from a random page of a book written to mean absolutely whatever one wants it to mean, and that what she read meant exactly whatever she wanted it to mean. I'm also un-amazed that she's using a divination book that's supposed to tell one the future as if it were a dictionary of spiritual characters. I wonder whether she was reading from the I-Ching at all or just inventing her own stuff. I can't say.

Soon I forget about this and my mind moves to other curiosities and I find myself imagining how high up we are right now, on the top floor of a building, the rain rushing down around us, just a hollow column of stone standing against the weather and the cold. I think of Paris extending out from us, our legs stretching down and out to become the roads and alleys, our arms the walls and rooftops, my eyes this window I'm facing, a collage of rippling, watery impacts. I think of the tide of people passing below us, a moving line of varying intensity, moving out from the doorways and running, newspapers clutched above, or brandishing colourful umbrellas stolen from here or there, taken, borrowed. In another part of my mind I feel an arm around me, it's warm — Neva seems to be snuggling up to me. Henry is still slumped in the corner. Ana has rolled over to the fridge — she's moving things in the fridge, dropping things on the floor, cursing in some alien or ancient language I can't recognise.

"So how do you like Paris… Capricorn?" Ana says, finally rolling back into view, holding a bottle of whisky and another spliff she must have pre-rolled and unearthed from its hiding place. Neva sits up, her heavy steel bracelets jangling as she takes the bottle to her mouth.

"Well…" I search for something suitably poignant to tell her. "It's pretty wet," I say. "There's so much rain it feels like the end of the world. But it feels that this the right place for the world to end."

"The world isn't ending" Neva scoffs. "Mars isn't in Scorpio and the signs haven't been picked up clear enough — I say we've got three more years to wait; three and a half at least."

"I don't even know what that means," Ana says earnestly, "The world ending, I mean. How would that work? How would it be, this whole world ending thing? We can't all drown, could we?"

"Well... No, not drowning. I don't think so," Neva says. "But the sun could go out and we could all freeze, or a meteor could hit the earth, or a supervolcano could erupt and everything would freeze when the ashes block the sun, or they could make a black hole in that CERN machine that would swallow the whole earth, or ISIS could release some deadly extraterrestrial bacteria and we'd all be dead in our sleep, or they could even hijack the CERN thing and fuck things up big time. Or it could be the Russians and their friends starting a nuclear war. You know: the possibilities are endless..."

"Hmm, and we'd never know what happened... When the end of the world comes... If it did, we'd never know what happened..." Ana muses thoughtfully, lighting her spliff and taking a long drag.

I just look from one to the other as they speak, watching their lips move.

"How do you mean?" Neva asks

"Well say ISIS made a black hole with that giant underground machine. They wouldn't have time to make a news report so we all knew it had happened. We'd just suddenly notice that everything was being sucked towards some black spot on the horizon while these guys celebrate shooting their AKs to the heavens — is that what happens with black holes?" Neva nods knowingly. "Or," Ana goes on, "say there was a supervolcano, the sky would just go black from the ash and there'd be tidal waves. But whatever happened, if we were killed, we wouldn't know what state the world was in afterwards. So we'd never know whether the world had really ended or not. We'd just know, in our last moments, that something had killed us. For all we knew it could just be some big storm that killed us, a bombing — as you say —, a gas explosion, maybe some old satellite falling on our apartment. But it might just be us who die. Then it wouldn't be the end of the world but the end of the world for us. And even if it was a really big event, there might be survivors and we'd never know once we were dead. When the end of the world does really come, we'll never know that's what it is. No one ever knows anything, to be fair."

Neva looks a little troubled by this. I too, had always somehow considered the end of the world to be some kind of final grand spectator event that I'd be able to witness, eating popcorn, pint in hand. I had never contemplated fundamentalists and extraterrestrial bacteria or apocalyptic machine-made black holes or varieties of all these. I take a swig of whisky.

"And anyway," Ana goes on, "it wouldn't be the world that was destroyed — it would just be the things that live here, society and stuff like that. There'd still be a big piece of rock floating through space, probably with tiny microbes on it that would eventually grow into new lifeforms. And everything would start again."

"Cockroaches," I offer, dredging up some nature documentary memory, realising she has moved from the bombings and politics to a more natural kind of catastrophe.

"It could be anything!" Ana says excitedly. "Maybe those weird deep-sea angler fish that look like alien monsters. Then people from other planets might eventually land here and be like, 'this alien life is fucking weird and gross like in our alien comic books,' but they'd just be seeing deep sea fish we'd known about for ages, and they'd never know we existed unless they found our bones, that's if we weren't all vaporised in the cataclysm!"

"I think," Neva says cautiously, "that the end of the world will be more of a mental thing. As in, you suddenly realise that everything is an illusion and that your consciousness is actually the whole universe. Like waking up out of a dream. There are films already talking about this kind of awakening. Because this is what this is: an awakening. We aren't really talking about the end of the world here but of the end of the world as we know it." She gives us an authoritative look and sits up slightly. "In Tibet," she says, apropos of nothing, "monks practice saying two sounds that release the soul from your body, up through the skull. Two syllables. So when you're about to die, you release your soul and it can go freely on to another body."

"What are the sounds!" Ana asks, excited.

"They're like *hoh* then *heee*," Neva says. The first sound is supposed to like open the top of your skull a bit, and the second sound is meant to disengage the soul from the body. The monks have to be careful practicing — usually they only practice the first syllable, because if they get them exactly right, they die!"

"*Hoh. Heeee*," Ana says, carefully.

"*Hoh. Heeee*," Neva says, smiling, living dangerously.

They stop and both look at me expectantly.

"*Hoh. Heeee*," I say, with poor conviction.

And then we sit there together, playing Tibetan roulette for a while. It occurs to me that this type of discussion is their bread and butter, and I am a privileged guest in their arena of mindless cosmic pondering.

At some point we all fall asleep.

§

I come back to my senses. Henry is still slumped in a corner. Neva and Ana are spooning by the coffee table. It's still raining. Everything dictates that I should be confused about waking up in this strange place but I actually feel like coming back to a long-established habit, as if I had been trained into this role, as if I had found a story in which I'm comfortable and where everything made sense. And yes, somehow everything makes sense — Neva and Ana, Henry passed out, the rain, the smell of onions on my jacket. Perhaps these aren't memories but the type of feelings one gets when things are starting to gel together. In other words: I feel well, rather well. And it feels like it's been a long time since I felt well.

I get up and head towards the kitchen, if you can call it that. The sink is packed with dirty plates and glasses. There are no cupboards or furniture save for an oven and a trash bin — they must keep all their dishes dirty to keep them somewhere. I drink straight from the tap and don't even make an effort to fix my eyes on the abandoned washing-up, should a rodent or some other creature be staring at me from the depths. It would be perhaps fitting to brew something but I might as well drink water from the toilet, instead of putting water in that rusty and greasy kettle. My stomach starts to feel queasy and I go back to the lounge. I search for the joint in the ashtray and find a leftover big enough to keep me busy for a while. I light the joint and puff away, lying on the floor, watching the rain bounce on the glass. It bounces like rain should bounce and then it's dragged downwards by the miracle we call gravity. There's nothing out of the ordinary in anything.

"You need to move in here," says Ana suddenly, barely opening her eyes.

"Good morning. Afternoon. Evening. Whatever," I say.

"Good whatever, Capricorn. You need to move in here. Really. It's been a while since we've slept like this."

"I have this effect on people," I say, "yes."

"No, really. A balance has been repaired," she says. "I can't explain it. It's as if a missing piece had been found — the puzzle is now complete. It feels like some web had been repaired by your presence. Some kind of web. Maybe the web of time."

"That sounds important. I mean, the repaired web."

"Let's go." She stands up on her rollerblades and walks all the way to the front door — I hadn't realised she was still wearing them. She motions for me to join her. I put the joint off on the coffee table and go after her. "Now, I need your help," she says, "help me down the stairs, please."

"Get on my back," I say.

"Really?"

"Yes! Go on."

She jumps on my back and I wrap my arms around her legs and back to the front. She's light — I can't barely feel her weight. She grabs my hair with both her hands and laughs.

"Hi-Ho, Silver! Away!" she says and I set off down the stairs, leaving the Yukio Mishima sticker behind.

I'm still stoned and I have a lapse of unconsciousness all the way down the stairs. Suddenly we are at the ground floor and it's still raining.

"Grab an umbrella from the corner," says Anna.

"Which one?" I ask.

"Just grab any!" she says.

I grab a red, white and blue umbrella, thinking it would be fitting to walk under the Parisian rain with a patriotic umbrella, even if this would make me a more likely target for a terrorist attack.

"I got the French one," I say. Ana laughs — she seems in a very good mood.

I walk towards the exit with Ana on my back and open the door. I try to offload her but she stays. I shake her off a couple of times but she doesn't seem interested in getting off my back.

"You won't get off my back will you?" I ask, redundantly.

"Are you mad?" she says and just stays there.

I bend my knees slightly and cross to the other side, careful of not banging Ana's head against the top of the door frame — I feel as if I were carrying a child, care must be taken, dangers must be avoided, for she wouldn't be able to do this herself, patronising as this might sound. I pass the umbrella to her and she opens it quickly and soon we are protected by a red, blue and white canopy with CARREFOUR, in reverse.

"Where to?" I ask.

"Over there," says Ana and she points with her right index.

I walk towards the corner, crossing people also covered by umbrellas that unavoidably bang against ours, that shake Ana on my back and shake me. It's as if people had no faces under the rain — as if people were only this or that other colour and brand, this or that product shouted into the void, from a band of 180, 200 centimetres over floor level. This has to be the biggest coup in marketing history, this free umbrella thing.

"What's this branded umbrella fad? Is it something like a government initiative, like the bikes for rent or something like that?" I ask. Ana doesn't reply. Maybe she hasn't heard me. Maybe she has no answer to this.

"Turn left here," she says instead and pulls the hair on the left side of my head. I turn there and keep walking. More people. More rain. A car drives past and splashes water and my feet are now wet. I can feel Ana's legs gluing to my arms and I can feel the heat of her body against mine. And her breathing. I get aroused by this contact. I feel like I'd like to smell her, just sit for hours and hours and smell her feet, her neck, her crotch, her hair; smell her wet clothes and her dirty and abused rollerskates. I don't even know where this feeling comes from. I guess I'm confused. Confused by something or someone or just acting on an impulse, mine or someone else's. "Here, boy!" she says and pulls my hair back from both sides. Now I want to smell her even more. I want to smell her. Not fuck her. Just lay down somewhere warm, smell her and feel her alive and breathing and doing the things the living do, which always imply some form of smell or other.

Now she's leading me to a café.

I push the door and walk in with her still on my back. Inside it isn't raining. Nor is it smokey — it's been a while since it's no longer OK to smoke indoors in Paris and considering the foul smell of the place I can't help thinking that a lot has been lost in ambience but also in narrative terms — a smokey café would have certainly been more interesting than this unremarkable albeit stinky joint. The patrons aren't unremarkable, though. They are mostly Arabs and without exception they are all looking at us, making it clear we have crossed a threshold we shouldn't have crossed, invaded a territory, a home under siege. Most likely, we just look like a fucking mess.

Ana seems unfazed by the eyes resting on us right now and sits at the first table available, she drops on it to be precise, and her right skate hits a table leg and a napkin holder falls to the floor. I pick it up, place it back on top of the table, and take the chair next to her.

"Thanks, Rohypnol," she says.

"Is this your local?" I ask.

"First time I've been here," she replies.

A stocky Arab man wearing brown trousers and a white shirt and blue apron, his age indeterminate, a moustache dictating a determinate manhood but not much else, comes to our table, stands before us with his hands on his pockets, and a rather beautiful smile

— staged or real — on his hairy face.

"*Bonjour,*" he says.

"*Bonjour,*" I reply.

"*Bonjour,*" says Ana, "*Je veux un jus d'orange et il veut un café, noir, bien sûr,*" she says.

"*Parfait,*" says the man and walks away.

"I've ordered for you," says Ana. "I sort of, somehow, knew what you wanted."

"Thanks," I say. This sounds like the most normal thing in the world, right now.

"Right," says Ana.

"Right," I say.

"So…"

"So what?"

"Are you moving in with us?"

"I'd love to but I've already paid for a week in advance at the hotel."

"Really?"

"Yes. It's the first time they've charged me in advance… I've been here other times… Never before have they charged me in advance," I go back to the same pathetic moan.

"Parisians have got extremely paranoid in these last months. They might want to cash in as much as possible before the end of the world. Even in the face of the Apocalypse — which as you know is just around the corner, even if Neva doesn't think so — they can't stop acting like Parisians, thinking about money…"

"You really think that will happen, don't you?"

"I have no doubt! Look at this weather, look at the songs on the radio, the politics, the demons knocking at the door…" She suddenly becomes forlorn, stares at her skates. She means it, really, even if the other one disagrees. And the phrase "demons knocking at the door": I've heard it elsewhere. I've heard it somewhere but I can't remember well where but it doesn't matter. "That's why you have to move in with us! Are you staying only for a week?" she adds.

"To be fair, I don't know," I say. "That hasn't been established yet. Nothing has been decided. Anything could happen, I guess," I guess.

"Do you have to go back to London for work? For something?"

"I don't know that either!" I say.

"It's a bit lazy, don't you think?"

"What?"

"All this lack of details. Lazy. This need to keep things to yourself. Here's another story about a guy without the burden of work, family — just a middle age guy in Paris with no real reason to be here."

"I know. I feel the same way. But I also think things could turn out quite good. Why do you need to know more than you know? I haven't asked much you either," I say, thinking about Neva as well.

"Yes, things could turn out well, I have no doubts about that! But we will have to take charge of it in some way, even if it means taking charge of the details. There must be some form of agency that can be reclaimed: the bull must be taken by the horns and a space of action must be reclaimed," she says, making very little sense to me, as the waiter places an orange juice and a black Americano on our table. I wanted to drink coffee, I guess. Ana thought so, so that must be the case.

We stay half an hour or so at the bar, Ana playing with her mobile phone and I staring outside and drinking my coffee, which seems to last an eternity, almost as if I were drinking from a magic cup. Either that or we don't stay in silence for so long and I'm exaggerating the duration of the scene. But regardless of how much time passes, the rain falls against the window and cascades down in streams that deform the people passing by outside, giving them a liquid aura. It has a hypnotic effect. Every now and then a man hidden under a branded umbrella — some unrecognisable brand, with characters belonging to some foreign alphabet — struggles to get through the door, betrays surprise when he sees us, further surprise when he sees Ana's skates, then joins a table with other men or just drops onto the first chair and grabs a paper and starts reading. Or they'll stare at us for a couple of minutes, make some comments in their own language we can't understand, and then move to other distractions, because even if alien we aren't that interesting, neither of us is either that good-looking or that ugly, and we aren't French, and therefore it's not easy to hate us either, even if we were until not too long ago speaking in English.

We finish our drinks.

I get the bill.

When we leave Ana jumps back on my shoulders and I carry her to the flat in Rue St Maur, all the floors up. We cross the door and we don't speak again. She disappears through a door next to the kitchen — so there was the toilet. In the living room Neva and Henry are still sleeping, rolled into balls, Neva hugging a cushion and Henry holding a shoe in his left hand. When Ana comes out, I gesture to her that I want to leave, shaking my right hand in upward and downward motions chest-height.

She sees me to the door. Outside, we arrange for me to come back tonight for dinner. She insists I should move in with them. Then she says something in a language I don't understand — there is a Latin root there, but I can't get it: it could be actually Latin for all I know. And then she closes the door on my face and I'm left there, staring at Yukio Mishima — the unhinged narcissist — once more.

§

I walk to Belleville station under the rain and then into a packed platform full of people of all races and creeds, with wet clothes and closed colourful umbrellas in their hands, waiting. There are a good 20 centimetres of water on the tracks and I wonder how the trains can work like that. But it seems they do, because soon the lights of a train illuminate the tunnel at the other end and the face of the driver, a woman wearing dark glasses, approaches me at high speed. There are no waves when the train finally stops in front of me.

I get on, pushing behind a group of soaked hipsters that smell of musty clothes and tobacco and avocado and I travel bouncing against people, stepping on people, smelling wet people and rubbing against people, thinking that a blast could kill us all, that it's only a matter of time until a blast kills us all, or until one of Ana's or Neva's apocalyptic catastrophes end us all, or only end me. Maybe there will be a blast and I'll die and everything will end here, or carry on with the other characters, like they said, like in that film about a blob from outer space, where the guy who seemed to be the main character gets killed ten minutes into the film. Or like *Psycho*. The world would carry on around me, the ads would change on the billboards in the station we've just passed, history would continue, but I wouldn't know.

When I get off at Pigalle to change to the line 12 I've already made my mind up that I'll pack my bag and move in with them. I might as well move in with them. It doesn't make sense but as anything could happen any time, as we could all be dead the next second, I might as well do it.

Take some chances.

Tick the box of having done something incredibly stupid, in Paris. Some new stupid thing in Paris.

Fall in love. Move in with them.

Fall in love with them both.

Live in a marriage of three. Quit whatever my job is in London, over text message. Or don't even bother. Come back only to pick up my stuff, or not come back at all and let the house be repossessed by the bank, if I own a house. Find a part-time job in some bar. Wait for the end of the world in Paris.

The bomb doesn't goes off — this time — and soon I'm back in the rain and soon I'm back in the hotel.

After sleeping for two or three hours I'm leaving my room again, this time forever: I'm never coming back to this hotel. Never again. Not now, nor ever. Before I close the door behind me I get a glimpse of Stephan in his room on the other side of the garden, talking to someone, waving his arms. He waves his arms a lot. He might start flying. Then he moves to the curtain, looks through the window. He doesn't see me but closes the curtain.

I leave.

CRUE DE LA SEINE 1910. — PARIS - Le Zouave du Pont de l'Alma au plus fort de sa crue.

3.

Leaves stamped on the sidewalk, as if etched. Crushed snails and squeezed slugs. Cigarette packs turned into a colourful mud, and Metro tickets, and newspapers' pages, and leaflets from some populist right wing organisation, claiming the arrival of their time, the moment in which they seize power, the end of the past order, the birth of the new one, call it a manifesto. And umbrellas bumping into other umbrellas and feet splashing muddy water on trousers, nylon tights, and shoes. No sign of birds. Not many tourists about. The Seine flows in the same direction. Even as it begins to spill from its banks into little squares and crooked streets.

§

It's now late in the afternoon. I'm not supposed to remember the code number to open the door but I do remember it, in what can only be some kind of glitch. I key in 6831 and the front door opens. I leave my bright mustard Renault umbrella with the rest of the umbrellas and climb the five floors to their flat. The door is open and I enter without announcing myself. Neva is typing on her keyboard although words don't materialise on the screen, so she might be banging keys for the sake of it, with the laptop off, and Henry is still slumped in the same corner. There's no trace of Ana. There's a strange mist in the flat.

"Hi Capricorn," says Neva without turning around. "I'm glad that you're moving in with us!"

"How did you know that?" I ask, genuinely surprised.

"I read an earlier draft of this chapter," she says, pointing at the blank screen.

"Oh, I see," I say, disappointed. "Any idea of how this continues?"

"I only read the part when you packed your bags in the hotel, having had the insight that it was in your interest to move in with us, probably in the hope that you might get something from us in return for the somnolence you bring: maybe sexual favours — men tend to think along these lines… I think it was a larger part in the previous draft and that it has been replaced by an ellipsis. The sexual ideas have also been edited out."

"I'm glad. And yes, it's quite elliptical now," I say, playing along.

"By the way, I'm worried about Henry," she says and finally turns around. She's wearing a pair of thick, black frames without lenses, a perfect match for her writing without words. Did she have lenses in her frames before? I can't remember.

"He's still sleeping…" I move next to Henry and

give him a few light kicks. He moans, moves his legs, but keeps on sleeping. I kick him harder. He moans harder, moves his legs again, doesn't wake up. I put my shoe on his head and pretend to step on him first, and then actually step on him, quite hard, but he doesn't moan or move his legs any longer. Neva witnesses my intervention holding her frames with her left hand. "He always wakes up by the time I step on his head," I say. "Should we call an ambulance, shove him in a cold bath, dump him in some back street, into some industrial bin, for him to wake up tomorrow with a missing kidney, or too late to escape a certain death crushed by a rubbish compacter?" I ask, all high spirits.

"I think we can wait a bit more before we take any desperate measures," says Neva. She's right, we can wait.

"You're right, we can wait," I say and just as I say this Henry starts puking to the side, slowly, silently, nonchalantly. It's more liquid than puke — some kind of liquified food, to be precise — that's leaving his mouth, dripping on the floor. "He's puking on your carpet!" I say.

"Let him do it. He'll get better," she says and turns around and starts typing again. The laptop's screen remains dark and motionless. Henry throws up a bit more and then jumps to a sitting position. He scans the room, confused. Then lies down again, this time on top of the puke.

"He lay down on top of the puke!" I cry.

"Stop worrying so much, Capricorn!" says Neva without turning around. Maybe she's right, maybe I'm worrying too much. Maybe I don't need to worry at all. "Let me finish here and we'll discuss the living arrangements," she says and turns briefly around to throw the hashish tin across the room in my direction. I'm already having second thoughts about moving in with people who are OK with Henry throwing up on the carpet. I'll move in anyway, though, as I have already made my mind up that I won't be coming back to the hotel. And once I make my mind about something there's no turning back.

§

Henry wakes up an hour or so later, after I have successfully rolled and smoked another massive joint. I'm once again stoned out of my head, reclining against a large purple cushion, watching the rain from my now usual upside down perspective, anticipating what will probably be my life from now on. The drops hit the glass, then move upwards and disappear behind the flower pots. When Henry comes back to the world of the living it's his time to worry — nobody likes to wake up to vomit. I find his expression of upside down consternation too funny to resist and I can't repress a pang of laughter. I can hear Neva giggling too. I sit up.

"This is fucking tragic..." says Henry, humiliated.

"It's hilarious!" I shout.

"Boys, boys, just relax," says Neva. "I'm trying to think here."

"I'm covered in sick!" cries Henry, looking in horror at his shirt, his jeans, the carpet. "What time is it?"

"It's tomorrow," I say. "It's tomorrow from yesterday."

"Now let's clean this mess," says Neva and she gets up and leaves the table and walks into the kitchen.

"I can't believe you let me make a mess of myself," says Henry, hurt.

"You heard the lady: relax." Henry stares at me. Although relatively stupid, his eyes have enough power to pierce my stoned mind. He's really pissed off. "Listen, mate, nothing to do with me. When I came back you were already covered in puke. We let you sleep it off. She said we should let you sleep it off."

"Came back from where?"

"From breakfast! From the hotel!"

"Is it really tomorrow?"

"Yes, dude! You slept for half a day. Maybe more."

"Fuck!"

"Yes."

"I was supposed to be somewhere else!"

"Where?"

"Somewhere."

"Really?"

"Yes. Somewhere else. Now I'm stuck here."

"Well, you shouldn't have smoked so much," I say and move to the ashtray and dig out the butt. I light it.

"Stop smoking that shit," he says. "It makes me sick."

"Whatever," I say. I smoke anyway.

Neva comes back to the room. She's carrying a mop and a couple of towels. She throws the towels Henry's direction and then mops the carpet. The carpet is already covered in stains and now is covered in stains and wet. She mops for a minute or two, while I watch her smoking and Henry rubs the towel in his clothes.

"I can't go home like this," he says.

"Capricorn can lend you some clothes," says Neva.

"True," I say. I put the butt out in the ashtray and make a move to my bag. I open the zipper and dig out the hoodie and the pair of sweatpants I use to sleep in. I throw both items of clothing in Henry's direction. He grabs the sweatpants by a leg and the hoodie falls on his lap.

"This is spiteful," he says. "You want me to dress like this? You want me to dress in this shit?"

"Sorry, dude. I left my two piece suit in London!" Neva laughs. Henry stares at us both, venom piercing through his thick glasses.

"Fuck you, guys!" he says. I feel he could start crying any moment. I don't quite get it, why he feels so strongly against tracksuits but I sense the need to slow down a bit.

"Hey, Henry: it's fine. We can get a cab to yours, get you properly dressed before we hit the road."

"Where are we hitting the road to?" he asks.

"Yes, where are we hitting the road to?" asks Neva.

I sincerely have no clue why I've implied we'll be going anywhere. I live here now, supposedly. I'm about to say something inviting everyone to forget what I have just said, or perhaps even inviting everyone to go out for a walk under the rain, to find a nice warm café somewhere quiet, talk about books and films, the sort of things that interest me not at all but that I have to pretend to care about in order to live up to what is expected of someone involved in something that takes place in Paris, when a loud bang announces Ana's arrival. Obviously she's wearing her skates, and slides from the door to my end of the room and drops to my side.

"Hi everyone… Sorry I'm late." I think "late for what?" "Late for the news!" she says, as if she had read my mind.

"What news?" asks Henry.

"It's happening! Do you understand? It's happening! TONIGHT!"

"YES!" shouts Neva. Henry and I look at each other. I have no idea of what she's on about. It's clear that Henry doesn't either. We have no fucking idea about anything.

§

Two hours or so later we're opening a trap door in Boulevard de Belleville. I'm opening it, to be more precise. Henry, Ana, and Neva just stand around me, Henry — dressed in my hoodie and sweatpants — holding two umbrellas, one in each hand, doing the best he can to spare me from the rain. We are all peering into the dark and deep void. Apparently we're heading to some underground party. Not underground in the sense of *indie* or any of those stupid words that mean nothing at all — underground as in *subterranean*, as in physically under the ground. And I'm doing the digging, metaphorically, for I'm just pulling from a piece of metal, trying to get a lid out. I don't necessarily buy any of this but I'm happy to play along, convinced that they'll tell me it was a lot of bullshit by the time I actually manage to pull the lid off, perhaps even before. But they don't tell me it was a load of bullshit while I pretend I can't lift the lid, for several minutes, so I might as well just make the effort and pull it out and throw it to the side.

"Right! Are you happy now?" I say, expecting them to start laughing ha ha and then we can all go back to their flat and figure out where the fuck I'll sleep until I go back to London, which will probably happen sooner that I was expecting, because leaving the hotel to which I can't go back because I've made up my mind I won't was clearly a stupid idea and these two — these three, for Henry should be included here too — are a bunch of delusional cunts.

"Yes!" says Neva. "Thanks a lot Capricorn!"

"You should leave the lid closer to the hole," says Ana and starts going down the ladder, "so that it's easier to put it back on." She goes down with her umbrella still open, without a single hint of a doubt, betraying certain familiarity with the task — it's clear she has been here before, she has gone down this hole before; for whatever reason, she clearly has gone down this hole before. Neva follows after her, also without closing the umbrella.

"Pull the lid back on the way down, Capricorn, we don't want to give this away," she says and suddenly

Grey Tropic

I'm watching the Air France logo on her umbrella disappear into the darkness below. I stare at Henry, I guess with horror in my eyes. His face betrays nothing — my guess is that he's still stoned.

"This shit's for real?" I ask.

"Seems so," he says, hands me my umbrella, closes his, and starts going down the hole too — even an idiot like Henry has more agency than me tonight.

He moves carefully down, holding the side rail with his left hand, not so proficient in his de-escalating skills, but still with some assertiveness that strikes me as quite unlike Henry. Now I can't be sure whether they have been here before, or this is déjà vu, in which they come across as having been here before when the truth is that they have never been here before. I know that all of this is very strange, that it hasn't stopped raining since I arrived — very unlikely in Paris — but there is a certain David Lynchian edge to the situation we're in that feels completely outside of space and time, for this is 2018 and not the late 80s. And maybe it isn't even a Lynchian turn that motivated their — my? — actions but writerly clumsiness or the need for something to happen. Every story can fall victim to the need of that story to be heard, seen, read, and even imagined. And only the stories where something happens, when a series of events leads to a certain interpretation, and that interpretation — more often than not — condenses into a moral, those are the stories that are read, heard, seen, and more importantly: remembered. Henry looks up as his face keeps sinking down.

"Coming?" he asks and shakes me out of my literary ruminations. I guess I have to follow them, these three lunatics, these three idiots. And this is exactly what I do, after throwing my umbrella to the side, a bulky red thing with a wooden handle, sponsored by Evian — *Evian: vivons jeune*.

I sit on the gash of the hole, my legs hanging down the abyss, on the opposite side to the ladder. My arse gets wet, of course, but not as wet as I had imagined it would. I grab the left side of the side rail, put my feet on the top rung and transfer my body to the ladder. I go down a few rungs. And then going down follows a certain instinct. My body is swallowed whole. While I'm still within reach I pull the lid to the centre of the hole and close it, after struggling to pull it into place for quite a while. The noise of the metal rubbing the cement reminds me of a late night in 1994, when I was completely off my head on acid and decided to write a message to who knows who on a wall, using an iron rod — the sound of the rod on the wall, it reminded me and my stoner friends of the sound of an opening tomb; the night descended into existential angst, just as I descend here. The lid feels heavier handled from underneath, and I wonder whether I'd be able to push it open without falling and breaking my back — what good would I be to a story about depths, crippled, unable to move, floating on a wheelchair down the Seine, like a poor cork abandoned to the water from the Pont des Arts, on a Sunday afternoon, those afternoons where students and tourists get together to eat and drink — careless afternoons of hope, breeders of future disappointments. And soon the lights penetrate the bars in the lid and draw a pattern on my clothes, and I guess on my face too — they draw broken patterns on the walls.

I move slowly down. I can hear the sound of Henry's shoes banging against the rungs, and Neva and Ana talking further down, the echoes of their voices climbing up, their strange language — an alien glossolalia only they seem to understand, making the moment even more strange.

"Just a bit more," I hear Henry's voice saying. I keep going down, reach the final rung, move my feet down and back, and soon I'm standing on a depression in the floor, both my feet in at least two centimetres of water — luckily my shoes are squeaky but still water proof, or are they, no they aren't, not any more.

Fernando Sdrigotti & Martin Dean

I look up: a big stream of water is falling to my right. Water drips on me, on everything — everything is wet. The water doesn't really rain in as it falls down the hole, splashing in bursts against the rungs, making a terrible noise when it reaches the bottom, like a gigantic and angry stream of piss. It isn't raining — rain doesn't penetrate the hole. It's the overflow water dripping from the sides that pisses in here, that it cascades in here. It must be something to do with the difference of pressure — I've seen something like this in the Pantheon in Rome: it was raining torrentially outside and the water didn't penetrate the hole at the top of that roof. Why all these memories, by the way? And where is all this water going? Where are we going? The second question is of course more urgent than the first one. I never thought I'd find myself disappearing into Paris' digestive apparatus, analysing the rain falling on me, not falling on me, the water, whatever, having flashbacks about trips to Rome, remembering the acid 90s, fantasising about being wheelchair-bound. I think it would be accurate to say it is at this point that I worry and perhaps even get scared, that all this could end up being more serious than I thought it would be. One is never prepared for anything serious when one gets thrown into someone's imagination (or lack of it).

When my eyes get used to the dark of these depths

I see Neva and Ana standing against a rusty metallic door. There's a weak lightbulb flashing — of course it's flashing, it could only be flashing — on top of the door and the light is not even strong enough for a disco-light strobe effect. Henry is looking around — to the sides, upwards, downwards, to his shoes, my tracksuit — he's wearing a tracksuit and brogues: how's that for ridiculous? Now he comes across as confused as me. If he had an idea of what was going on just some moments ago that was a mere accident.

"Right. Now be quiet," says Ana and takes her right index to her lips in the universal sign for 'be quiet'. She knocks on the door. A metallic echo bounces off the walls on the other side. She knocks again, this time following some pre-arranged rhythmic pattern that sounds a lot like *La cucaracha*. I can hear the noise of feet dragging across the floor on the other side, the sound of a latch or a key in the door. A small window, not bigger than half an A4 piece of paper starts to open in the door — I hadn't seen the window before. When it finishes opening, a hand in a glove passes a mobile phone across the gap — the hand doesn't as much pass the phone as it drops it to our side. Ana gets the mobile phone and keys something in, I guess a number, and then drops the mobile phone back to the other side. I turn around to look at Henry but he's nodding off, with his head bouncing up and down trying to stay awake, looking like one of those dogs some minicab drivers in some places like to stick in the back of their cars, but also drooling, not a lot, but still drooling like an idiot — this sight makes me very angry and I feel like pushing him into the water but then I remember he's wearing my clothes so I change my mind.

The little window closes without much noise, without any noise. Some moments elapse, during which Ana turns around and looks at the three of us with a proud smile in her face; Neva looks at me too — her eyes are shining and she has a self-conscious smile on her face too and she looks incredibly pretty. It's clear they know what they are doing, that they are now in command, that they now own this shit, and that maybe that touches some sexist or chauvinist nerve in me and that I'm not very comfortable, not comfortable at all. Then a loud noise and something that sounds like someone playing with a big chain, and the door opens. From my angle I can't see who opens the door. But I can see Neva and Ana disappearing through it, out into the night that is on the other side. I bang Henry on his right shoulder with the back of my hand and he wakes up, startled. I move towards the door and cross the threshold. Henry follows behind. And soon we're standing against a rail, in a little elevated path in a dark tunnel not more than two metres high, with water running down the middle, looking like something out of *Ghostbusters II*, but without the pink slime. I think that soon my nose will be hit by the foul smell of what is by any standard a sewer but the water running below us, in the gut of the tunnel, seems to be rain water and not shit. There are weak lightbulbs on the walls, spreading all the way into the distance every three or four metres. A missing lightbulb can be spotted every now and then, before the tunnel bends towards the right and the lightbulbs and the water disappear who knows where to.

The person in charge of the door is a short old woman with a bob. "*Salut Agnès*" said Neva upon crossing the door — I have no reason to suspect she isn't called Agnès. She can't be taller than 140cm; she's wearing an elegant Jackie Onassis sort of dress, but floral, and has a huge smile on her face and my impression is that she's stoned — she must be in her 90s and stoned. And how did she manage to reach the window? Is there a stool hiding somewhere? Perhaps the mobile phone ruse is a practical one and not a gimmicky stunt; perhaps that's the only way she has to attend to the door, find out who's knocking. She waits for Henry to cross and then leans against the big metallic thing, almost twice her size, and pushes it with her back until it locks with a thud. And then she points toward the end of the tunnel, never stopping to smile for a second. Ana and Neva lead the group and the old lady walks at the back. And soon we disappear into the tunnel too.

§

We walk in silence, bathed by the weak light of the lamps. The noise in my head doesn't stop, the seemingly whimsical recollections keep popping up.

On a rainy night of August 2003, a group of anti-terror officers training in the catacombs of Paris bumped into what seemed to them either a practical joke or clear traces of terrorism. Who could imagine an underground secret society — underground in the physical sense — could exist in 21st century Paris? Not them, certainly not them. But the *Mexicaine de Perforation*, the *Mexicaine of Perforation* could and did and to this day exists underground, moving from this to that other corner of the vast gut of the Parisian catacombs. Enough. Enough. Enough. Make the intrusive thoughts stop.

The water runs smooth in the canal, almost noiselessly. Every now and then we walk under an area of leakage. Neva and Ana, walking to the front, have their umbrellas open. I turn around and Henry and the bobbed midget have theirs too. I'm the only one without an umbrella and my jacket is completely wet. But I prefer a wet jacket to the stupidity of carrying an open umbrella underground.

We walk and we have been walking for some minutes now, not sure how many. Every now and then we pass a dark and narrow gap in the wall — it's impossible to tell whether a door or just an indent in the wall or a tunnel leading to other parts of the sewers. When we get to another one of these gaps Ana stops. She moves to the side and Neva does too. The midget walks to the front and stands by the door. She takes a big set of keys from her purse, presses a switch on the wall and a light flashes in the gap, revealing another metallic door, pretty much like the one we crossed to get in. She shoves the key in the lock, opens, and then knocks, once like any mortal would, the second time once again with the beat of *La cucaracha*, yes, it's *La cucaracha*: ta ta ta ta taa ta ta ta ta taa ta ta ta ta ta ta taaaaa. She moves back. The door opens towards us and a big bald old guy with a funny conical head, wearing aviators and an M65 jacket, now stands before us, smiling.

"*Allez! Allez!*" says *Agnès*, inviting us to cross to the other side. We do. She crosses last. And then pulls the door shut behind her. As we move away from the door and into a dark room — the size of a tennis court — with a cinema screen in one end and at least a hundred people inside, some talking, most staring at the screen, with their backs to us. I can hear the sound of the keys and a latch closing behind me. The midget and the bald guy stay by the door, talking. Both move their hands a lot and I'm absolutely convinced they are discussing something important. Ana and Neva walk into the crowd and we follow them.

It's as if we were in a dream. It's as if I were in a dream. But we aren't in a dream, this won't end up being that artifice, it could not possibly be that, I'm pretty sure. We are in a story but we are very awake, and walking in this dark cavernous room, full of people from back to back, watching the black and white images projected against a giant screen, slow, methodically montaged together, a long time ago, every comma a comma further away from the moment in which these images were put together first. We walk through the crowd while on a screen a story is unfolding in French. The images on the screen don't move — they are photographs, played one after the other, while a man narrates, a raspy voice that betrays too many cigarettes. A man with a mask, something like a mask covering his eyes. Two men stare at him. The man with the mask contorts, suffers. Then a short fade to black.

Grey Tropic

A countryside scene, some horses visible, a couple of trees. A room full of light. A kid. Pigeons. A cat. A cemetery. An outdoor viewing pier in some airport. A boat in a misty day. A woman. Ruins. Another woman. Another woman, this one in the viewing pier, perhaps the same viewing pier, perhaps a different one. Perhaps the same woman. Maybe a different one.

"Hey, come this way," says Neva and grabs me by the elbow. She starts walking, pulling me towards her. I follow.

"What's that film?" I ask.

"No idea," she says. "They always screen the same one…" I try to turn around and watch the screen some more but she moves too fast in the opposite direction to the images. I don't struggle and walk faster. We bump into people without apologising. And we walk for what feels like an eternity but might be only a couple of minutes because the room isn't as big as to allow an eternity and eternity after all doesn't exist in fiction. Until there's fewer of them, fewer people. And until, much to my surprise, we seem to reach the end of the multitude and the end of the room, which doesn't end in a wall, but that opens to a sort of miniature amphitheatre, packed with an audience watching a man recite what I believe to be a sort of comic monologue — the audience is laughing,

laughing at the fat masked man — perhaps not that fat but rather bulky — shouting his lines wearing only a pair of speedos. We stand just before the seats, and his shouts mix with the narration of the film coming from the other end. If I understood French I'd feel dizzy.

"What the fuck is this place?" I ask Neva.

"Cool, isn't it?"

"I can't tell… I can't tell, to be fair… Where's Henry? Where's Ana?"

"I don't know. I lost them!" Neva stops by a large barrel. There are many of these scattered around. "Do you have some money, some small change?"

"Sure," I say. I give her a handful of coins. "What for?" She doesn't answer and puts her hand inside the barrel and soon takes it out dripping and holding two bottles of beer from the necks. Then she throws some coins in the barrel placing some others in her right pocket. And then she passes me one of the bottles — her hand is wet and cold.

"*Salut!*" says Neva unscrewing her beer; I open mine too. And then we toast banging our bottles, staring at each other's eyes — Neva isn't wearing her glasses — her eyes are dark and huge and beautiful. "It's a party, isn't it? What more do you need to know?" We move closer to the seats, sit on the top steps.

"This is an amazing venue," I say, looking around.

Grey Tropic

"Venue... What a horrible word, but yes, it's a nice venue. It's a secret one too. So don't go telling anyone how to get here."

"Who would I tell this to?"

"I don't know... Your readers?"

"I'm not the writer of this story!" I say.

"I thought it was a first person narration! Look: it's a first person narration. You've just said '*I'm not the writer of this story,' I say*," she says — she's sharp.

"Yes, true. But it's not autobiographical. I'm not the writer. Getting that wrong is a basic kind of mistake, Neva..."

"That's what all writers say," says Neva. "And—" a roar of laughter drowns the rest of her words. I take offence about this, because she's absolutely right.

"He seems funny... What's he's on about."

"He's telling a story about his strange neighbour, an Englishman who masturbates by the window, pulling and tugging his dick instead of doing it like all men do, whatever it is that you do, however you do it, because I haven't got a clue... Anyway, this same Englishman came to his room, he says, with a pair of shorts and his balls and cock hanging from the side, to argue some completely made up nonsense about a smell coming from his window. This is hilarious! He's funnier than me telling you. He says it's a true story."

"It sounds familiar. Is he a famous comedian?"

"First time I've seen him," she says. More laughter.

"I'm sure I heard this story before," I say. It rings a bell. I could have seen it in a film, read it in a book, I could have imagined it — it feels like déjà vu and I'm about to crack it, to figure where it is I've head when I feel a hand on my shoulder. It's Henry, drinking from two bottles of beer, both held with his left hand, why I don't know. Ana is here too and I realise for the first time tonight that she's not wearing her rollerskates now — maybe she isn't that crazy after all. Or was she wearing her skates earlier and I didn't notice? Is it possible to go down a ladder wearing skates?

"Hi guys!" says Ana. "Thought you had left!" Henry nods and drinks from one of his beers. They sit next to us, on Neva's side, just as the crowd starts clapping and the masked guy in his speedos walks out. The lights on the stage go off. And soon they go on again and a pair of guys walk in to the roar of the public, who are in a complicit mood, who know about this, who probably know these guys' lines by heart, who will find a lot in common. One them is dressed in an orange suit and has his hands shackled to his feet with a long chain — he has a shaven head and a goatee and reminds me of an actor but I can't really remember which actor. The other one is all dressed in black, wearing a balaclava, and has a large butcher knife. The one with the orange suit kneels and the one in black takes the knife to the prisoner's neck. I get ready for a mock execution, a critique of the contemporary need to document death with a camera, something incredibly contrived, boring, morally debatable, smug. Instead, the prisoner starts talking.

"*Rien à faire!*" he shouts. The public laughs.

"*Je commence à le croire! J'ai longtemps résisté à cette, pensée, en me disant, Vladimir, sois raisonnable. Tu n'as pas encore tout essayé. Et je reprenais le combat… Alors, the revoilà, toi…*"

"*Tu crois?*"

"*Je suis content de te revoir. Je te croyais parti pour toujours.*"

"*Moi aussi! Merde!*"

And here the mock execution happens at last, when the guy in black starts moving the knife in a violent sawing motion and blood starts squirting from the prisoner's neck, a fake bright red blood pumping out in a steady stream, all over the stage, and the audience in the first two or three rows of seats, who surge back in horror, not at the idea of being squirted by real blood but at the idea of their clothes getting soaked with that fluorescent, very likely cheap and toxic, liquid. Then the prisoner falls to the ground. And the executioner takes the knife to his own neck and starts cutting himself, in even more violent motions, and the blood starts shooting from his neck too, but this time it's blue blood squirting, going two metres up and then falling to the ground after tracing a short parabola. And then he collapses too. The lights go off. Someone starts clapping. But the lights go on again, soon, and the two guys are now standing in the middle of the stage, holding a white flag. Blood keeps squirting from their necks, and it falls on the flag — white, blue, red, I see what they are doing here, how very clever, how challenging and slightly politically incorrect, both executioner and executed painting the French flag with their respective bloods, wow! And just to confirm my criticism, just then they start singing *La Marseillaise*. The audience starts clapping and cheering, some even stand up to clap and join in the singing. The two men on the stage walk away, their loud voices still heard. The lights go off. The audience goes crazy. And I have no fucking idea of what I have just seen apart from the fact that it can only have been imagined by someone incredibly stupid.

When the lights go on again a black guy wearing a white apron is mopping the floor. A guy walks quickly into the stage, I recognise him. It's the dick twanger. He's not wearing his mask now but his speedos are still on and any other item of clothing is missing. He announces something in French, with his usual brisk manner and physical jolts — funny that he hadn't twitched delivering his monologue. But this seems to be something urgent. The lights go on in the entire place. The film stops playing. The audience starts getting up from the steps and walking up the stairs. Some start running. Meanwhile I'm processing the fact that he told a fake story, probably about me. Or that maybe I told a fake story. Maybe the dick twanger was me all the time. Was it? Did I twang my dick by the window? Was it me? I sincerely can't tell any more and this makes me very angry. I'm processing all this, with the people now running up the stairs, when I feel a pull from the back.

"Come on! We must leave!" shouts Neva and starts moving in the same direction as everyone else.

"What's wrong?"

"It will flood! The Seine has risen five metres in the last four hours. We need to evacuate!" I'm quite impressed by the accuracy of Neva's (and Stephan's warning). Impressed but not in shock — action is needed here and this action entails my leaving this place and leading my friends to safety, because that's the kind of guy I am.

I make a move and so does everyone else. Now

everyone is running towards the exit and so are we, the four of us. But because there's only one door we don't get far and soon we're all packed in the middle of the room, waiting for the others to leave. People are scared; I hear cries; the exodus will be slow. I start to fantasise about drowning, that I'll drown here, with all these unknowns, after having been accused of being a dick twanger, that I'll drown in the same room with a dick twanger, that I could even be said dick twanger, that I'll drown without sleeping with Neva, that I'll die before doing whatever it is I needed to do in this life, real or imagined (the life). What a terrible turn for this story. What an unnecessary death. What have I done to deserve this? I should have never listened to Neva and Ana. I should have gone back to London, to stories about misery and grey skies and rocketing rents, and people obsessed with shrinking their genetic pool when I had a chance. In all fairness this is all Henry's fault. I hope he dies a slower death than mine. I hope he drowns with a massive brown Parisian turd stuck in his mouth. I hope I get to see him drown. I hope I die only after seeing Henry squirt a brown turd through his nose.

Neva holds my hand — it feels warm. She pulls me, kisses me. We'll probably die like this. She tastes like tobacco and cafe latte, *café au lait*. Someone pushes us.

Grey Tropic

More people push us. The crowds seems to be moving. And soon we're out in sewers.

§

And we run. We're running in the sewers, the four of us, following a large group of fellow escapees. We must be twenty in total and we're running in the same direction as the water, that's splashing wild by our side. The rest have gone the other way, towards the entrance we used, perhaps; or perhaps they just used another exit. I spot Stephan in our group, leading in his speedos, the lying dick twanging bastard leading us into freedom — (this is a good omen, for some reason I can't put into words). And we run. We run as if we were racing the end of the world. And we probably are.

We run for 10 or 15 minutes. There's no room here for being physically tired, for exhaustion, for old age or any bodily constraints that would forbid this heroic escape. We run, solid and healthy, fast, very fast. This is certainly problematic and I'm sure we'll get in trouble about this if we manage to get out. Coming to think about it — as I make my escape from this place and the whole spatio-temporal continuum becomes flexible — the whole politics of this story is rather debatable. Where are the minorities in this story? I don't see any black people, any Eastern Europeans, any migrants from the Global South. Yes, there were some French Arabs in the café we went to with Ana but these were given a minor role as extras. But what am I? Have I been described? Am I really an Englishman or just happen to come from London? Did Stephan classify me with the precision of a Swiss clockmaker or did he misread me entirely? Why couldn't I be one of the myriad migrants coming to London from all over the world, finding a home in that unfriendly and grey city, now temporarily in Paris? What about my name? Where does such a name come from? Is that a real name or a nickname? Am I really named like a clothes washing liquid and a mermaid? WHO THE FUCK AM I? I'm so distracted by these thoughts that I don't even get surprised about the place we arrive to in our dramatic escape from the flooding intestines of Paris.

Imagine a gigantic upside-down funnel.

An upside-down funnel: a gigantic circular room made of bricks from bottom to top. A walking platform, elevated several metres above the water and accessible via stairs on both sides, goes all the way around the funnel. Distributed evenly, forming a cross of sorts, there are four metallic ladders going all the way up to four holes in the ceiling, some ten or twelve metres above — the central hole must be an air duct. The water — growing in volume and speed — disappears through three tunnels — this thing might distribute the water to different exits. We run clockwise around the platform, our footsteps amplified by the metal in the floor. The first ones to arrive at a ladder start climbing, five or six of them. Others stop to wait.

"*Utilisez les autres échelles!*" shouts Stephan, commanding, reminding me of Lee Marvin on *Big Red One*, beyond the language problem and the fact that he doesn't look like Lee Marvin at all and he's wearing speedos. But there is something of a war vet in him, something that leaves no space for doubt or fear, although his voice trembles. And what did he say? I guess it's something about using the other ladders too — that would make sense.

But I don't have time to linger on this and I continue running, followed closely by Neva and a bunch of people, now an amorphous mass, a faceless and nameless matter to which I have no connection at all save for the fact we want to get out of here together or alone, but we want to get out. I've lost visual contact with Henry and Ana, but I trust they are here too, maybe running counterclockwise, climbing some of the other ladders, like many others. When we reach the second ladder there are already four people using it. The third one is still vacant, we reach it and start climbing. We climb quickly, Neva after me — the water starts to get to the walkways. Suddenly shouts can be heard from our right: I turn around without stopping to get a glimpse of the fourth ladder, like a falling tree, all the way midstream into the water with four of five people attached to it. They go in and disappear below the surface and are taken by the current into the tunnels to their death, one can only guess. But our ladder doesn't give in and soon I'm pushing a lid like the one I had to pull to get us in here and I'm climbing another stair in a narrow tunnel — light can be seen at the end, several metres above. I turn around to see if Neva is following and she is. We climb as fast as we can and soon another lid that I push to the side without much effort and I'm out.

I help Neva out and we fall to the grass embracing. And we kiss again. She now tastes like tobacco and mud.

We stay there under the rain, while others exit the holes around us.

§

Soon the morning light starts to show its blue face,

behind the buildings that stretch into the distance. We're sheltering in what looks like a bandstand, in a mountain overlooking a park. We're in the highest part of the Parc des Buttes-Chaumont, a pretend ruin sort of building known as the Temple de la Sibylle, I've been informed by Stephan, who's shaking in his speedos to my left, cold and suffering or shocked to death, I don't know. He doesn't seem to recognise me and I'm not in the mood to remind him that it's him — yes, my mind doesn't betray me — who's the dick twanger. I'm preoccupied with more important things now and he looks afraid, like a wet harmless moustached kitten in speedos, a useless creature galaxies away from the Lee Marvin I imagined him to be when the panic made him become useful, perhaps for the first time in his life, and he lead the way out of the tunnels.

Where's Henry? Where's Ana? Did they make it before the water siphoned out of the exits as if Paris were a concrete whale reaching for air on the surface? Did they drown? But more importantly, how did we get here, so high? Did the ladders take us here? But did we climb so much? We seem to be in a very elevated part of the city and I only remember climbing a short stretch up, some ten or fifteen metres. And now it's the heights and we're watching the buildings from above. We're above everything except perhaps the Eiffel

Tower, that I can't see from here, so there's no way we could have reached this place straight from the tunnels. Do I suffer from short term memory loss? Am I in shock? Is this more authorial licence, another elision, or just bad writing? I look around: there must be ten of us. What happened to the rest? Numbers just don't add up. This has all the signs of something going wrong by accident or design. Neva is here, cuddled against me, wet from head to toe, cold and shaking too. I can't believe I'll never see Henry again; yes, he's dead. I can't believe all these people died or disappeared like this and no one bothered to dedicate at least a paragraph to them. Or a footnote. Or at least a convincing couple of sentences to account for their disappearances. They were rather useless and Henry was incredibly stupid but this is no way to kill your characters. The way things went, from being in the party to being here, watching Paris flood, seems unreal to me, and certainly perverse too.

And suddenly, as I'm busy pondering over my sad destiny as a character in yet another novel that takes place in Paris, a big ball of lightning crosses the skies from top left to bottom right. The sound is deafening and it reverberates across the city below. Suddenly a huge tidal wave, scratching the belly of the clouds up above, comes rushing from the distance, swallowing everything it encounters. I can even now see the doomed Eiffel Tower, dragged by the water, riding the waves in true Californian style. It'll be a matter of seconds before the wave swallows us too. I hear screams around me. Stephan jumps into the cliff to speed things up, shouting something incomprehensible in French. Some others follow him — *QUELLE MERDE!* they shout as they go, all very French. Only Neva and I remain. She pulls me close to her. I close my eyes and kiss her. And wait for my own death with my eyes closed, tasting her stale breath. It was bound to happen. It was everyone's time to go.

"*Quelle merde,*" she says kissing me.

"*C'est une merde, aussi,*" I say.

And then everything is over.

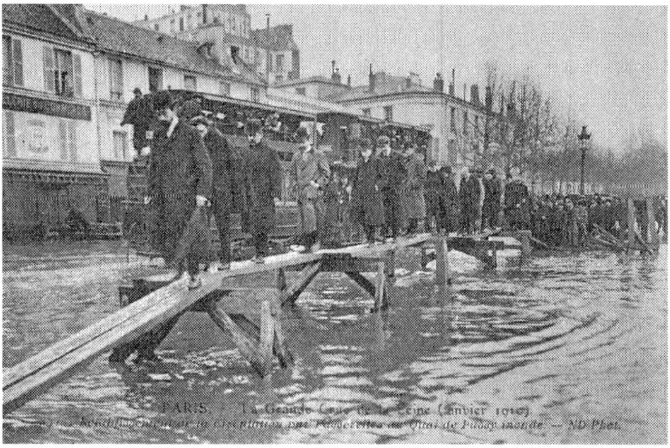
PARIS.
ND Phot.

4.

A pigeon, ill-looking and with one leg missing, is biting a snail. It pulls the snail out of its shell, all muscles and cartilages. The snail fights for a while, springing like jelly, desperate, before it is swallowed. It's a large bite but the pigeon doesn't choke. Then it bites some more at the now empty shell. And then it flies away and mixes with the other pigeons battering their wings below the dark alleys of Place des Vosges, stuffing their guts with the chewy delicacies the wet weather has gifted them with.

§

I can't begin to explain the disappointment of waking up in Neva and Ana's flat. I'm unwet and undead. Lying next to Henry, who's also alive and dry and unvomited, wearing his own clothes and his pathetic brown brogues and sucking his thumb. Here we are, two stoners paying the price of smoking a huge spliff, victims of the oneiric recourse, the number one killer of literature.

My head hurts and I'm still holding my lighter in my clenched right fist. What a terrible shit story this one has turned out to be. What a cheap and unnecessary ruse, the dream sequence. And not to mention all this fucking meta-fiction shit. How little imagination by the authors: so much contempt for the power of fiction to create possible worlds — unbelievable at first but sooner or later cemented into beautiful lines of flight, points of departure from everything that is mundane in real life. If there is any emancipatory possibility left in literature that is the creation of unbelievable worlds — all the rest is a form of surrender, particularly if we are talking about an assassination attempt against the suspension of disbelief. And this is a dream sequence that stretched for almost 8,000 words! I've been in shit stories before and this one won't be different, that much I know right now.

I repress a terrible drive to pronounce the death of the novel first, and then this thing here, this short story that went on for too long. Is this a novel, is this a *novella*? Whatever it is it has outlived its purpose. It should burn. In all fairness, all writing should be pronounced dead, set on fire. There is no daring in writing, no ideas left; nothing but typing and an unflinching and pathetic surrender to the imperatives of reality and realism and marketing, online presences, authorial websites, analytics and links leading to Amazon pages, writers saying incredibly stupid things on social media, all the time. It's all the same and if it isn't the same from the start it'll become the same sooner or later, in order to meet the demands of that tree-killing monster: the publishing industry.

Take this story, this *novella*, this thing, whatever you want to call it. Why couldn't it have embraced that almost magical realist turn? Why couldn't a story about Paris involve an apocalyptic end? Why couldn't a story about Paris entail a complete and unapologetic departure from reality? Was it the fear that the text would be accused of trying to run away from an already apocalyptic present, a present where the ones doing the killing aren't tidal waves but masked AK-wielding halfwits with a thirst for blood and immigrant-bashing right-wing turds and governments and and and? Is there a catalogue of realities from which one is allowed to escape? Was it the demand that a Parisian story adjusts to certain parameters of reality, certain parameters always dictated by scientific logic, even at those moment when the parameters feel bent, abused, irrelevant for this day and age? Was it the demand to plug into the idea of being *avant garde*, whatever that means, and we all know it means absolutely nothing? I don't really know. I only know that I want to press delete and move on to something new but something stops me from doing it — perhaps the fact that characters never get to decide the shape of the story which they are in, let alone the shape literature will take. How unfair. I don't even have access to that kind of suicide. What an absolute pile of shit. Or do I? I don't know.

I hear a noise to my left. Henry gets up, moaning. He takes his hand to his head, and then to his face; he looks around confused and then spots me and makes a face of even bigger disgust.

"What the fuck are you doing here?" he asks. "Fucking God…" he continues, holding his head.

"What do you mean? You got me here?"

"Did I?"

"Yes, dude! You brought me here!"

"You might be right…" he says. He reaches for the ashtray and scavenges for a butt. He lights it. Smokes. "You should be happy I'm not dead," he says.

"Yeah, true," I say. "But nobody dies of a weed overdose," I add.

"I don't mean this," he says and passes the butt my way.

"What do you mean then?"

"Your stupid dream!" he says. "All that apocalyptic bollocks."

"How do you know that?" I say and pass the butt his way.

"You don't read drafts, do you?"

"No, I don't. Never have the time."

"Well… In the previous draft the dream wasn't a dream."

"Are you sure?"

"Absolutely!" he says and smokes. Then crushes the butt in the ashtray.

"And what happened?"

"It didn't hold together! That kind of fantasy never holds together. Sooner or later it comes crashing down…"

"I don't mean why it was edited into a dream… I mean what happened after you — and presumably Ana too — died. What happened to Neva and I after we exited the sewers in that park, at the top of that mountain, in the earlier draft?"

"That didn't make much sense, did it?"

"No, it didn't. It didn't. Nice location though."

"Yeah, the location is nice, no doubts."

"So, what happened?"

"Well, to begin with you survived the tidal wave…"

"How?"

"Well, that wasn't clear in the draft. I think they left it for later or they just couldn't be arsed…"

"Another elision?"

"Maybe… Maybe there was an elision, and then — in one of the versions — Neva and you were rowing in one of the boats that are normally, supposedly, there in that park, in the little lake... You know, the boats people use to go around in circles in the lake, if they do, because I don't know if they exist... Anyway... You were rowing towards the Eiffel Tower and..."

"The Eiffel Tower?"

"Yes, the Eiffel Tower and..."

"The Eiffel fucking Tower! Can it get any more clichéd?"

"I didn't write it, mate. Should I continue?"

"Yes, but make it short. Why were we rowing towards the Eiffel Tower?"

"Hold on, this is very bad, almost a joke: because you were the Chosen Ones!" he snorts and starts laughing.

"THE CHOSEN ONES FOR WHAT?" I ask.

"To save humanity!"

"GET OUT OF IT!"

"I swear to God, mate, that this was the first version."

"Wow... That's very bad!"

"Yes... Awful."

"And why the Eiffel Tower?"

"That's an even worse cringe..."

"Can't it be any worse?"

"It can: you were rowing towards the Eiffel Tower to join the other Chosen Ones — people from all cultures and races who would be taken to other planets on the Eiffel Tower, that it's not a fucking lump of metal but a secret starship. You would escape to another planet, planet Mongo, somewhere in another galaxy, where the vibrations are different and there are no wars or hate, in order to start anew, and preserve the whole of the human race by reproducing all races and cultures over there… At least that would require getting laid, I mean…"

"You have to be kidding me!"

"No, man, it's true."

"Henry: who wrote this? A ten year old…"

"I told you it was a cringe."

"At least they put some *people from all cultures and races*. That was a nice touch, considering that this story is whiter than snow…"

"Tokenism… Just that. They thought they could shove in some brown people right there and get away with the rest of the story. But it didn't make sense, really. The starship thing didn't make sense. The editor cut it."

"Yes, it's impossible to make that work… I'm glad the editor has a brain here. And were there other versions?"

"Well, there were notes… Some vague things about possible routes that were never followed through."

"Like what?"

"Off the top of my head… In the other ending you

guys created a sort of anarchist commune at the top of the Parc des Buttes-Chaumont, using the bandstand as headquarters, in order to wait for the rescue. But the rescue never happened because you were the only people left in the world and so you are now charged with the survival of the human race— again — and so you learn how to fish and eat with the fruits and roots that you can find at the top of this park... and shag a lot, you had to shag a lot in order to repopulate the world. And you were there, living in those ruins, with that majestic and sublime view of the wrecked city from the top of that mini-mountain, a tiny affair à la Caspar David Friedrich."

"This makes even less sense... And it sounds potentially nazi and even incestuous."

"I don't think this went beyond some vague notes on a notepad... That said, all writers end up in nazism, if you give them enough time. I think there's a law about it... Goldman Law or something like this. I think it's a *meme*."

"Like the good progressive and liberal intellectual character that I am, I hear the word *meme* and I reach for my gun," I say, for no clear reason. "Anything else? Any other ending?"

"Apart from this there was one more option... Not that bad but too meta, even for this story."

"Tell me!"

"OK, you've asked for it!" Henry says and takes a deep breath. "In this route Neva and you survived the tidal wave and walked the streets of Paris looking for the writer of this story, in order to demand a happy ending, not in the sense of a handjob, but in the widely accepted expectation that stories end happily. How would this happy ending be arrived at, you would debate with Neva for pages and pages, walking down the streets of Paris? Perhaps the happy ending could arrive via some magical realist ruse, you guys concluded at some point…"

"That would have been nice!"

"Yes, no, who knows… it depends on the execution. In any case, the editor of the story — who in that version was the dick twanger you claim to have seen from the window of your hotel room — starts chopping pieces of text off because he resents having been turned into a cheap dick twanger. He also happens to hate meta-fiction and magical realism, and starts to turn this story into a run-of-the-mill but more readable Parisian story — it could even be argued that he turns it into a potentially successful Parisian story, or at least a better Parisian story, albeit one lacking any unique selling point. But as a result you and Neva start acting in ways that seem unnatural to you both. And of course you can do nothing about it because you are just a couple of characters."

"I like this!"

"Wait! It gets better! But how could you escape the ruthless hand of an editor? An editor not precisely compassionate to the need for the story to challenge the boredom of contemporary fiction? An editor concerned about book sales and good reviews? A fucking coward of an editor! How could you escape? How could you? HOW?"

"TELL ME!"

"SELF-PUBLISHING!"

"OH NO!"

"Yes! Self-publishing! The only possible way out of this story, the only possible way this story — had it continued that extreme meta road — could be published would have been self-publishing! Who would publish this otherwise? And with that in mind both you and Neva walk the streets of Paris, in love, having conversations that could easily belong in a shitty film by Richard Linklater, running against time and running away from the editor, trying to find a portal, hidden in one of the bookshelves of Shakespeare and Co — a portal that leads straight into the slush pile of a vanity press. And we all know how quickly that kind of slush-pile goes down…"

"Hmmm. I'm not sure about that portal thing…"

"Yeah, me neither… I guess that's why this version was ditched…"

"Portals never lead anywhere good. Unless they are written by Lewis Carroll, in which case they are also written by a paedophile."

"I like the idea of this story ending in Shakespeare and Co, though."

"Never been there. Is that the bookshop near Notre Dame? That one where people who can't read in French go to take pictures of books that they won't read in English?"

"That one. I'll take you one day," Henry says at the same time that the door opens and Neva and Ana walk in. Both are laughing, wearing dark shades, carrying some plastic bags, Carrefour bags, wearing raincoats, traces of rain all over their bodies and clothes. But I'm not in love with Neva; we have never kissed; we have never waited for death together at the top of the Parc des Buttes-Chaumont, waiting for a tidal wave to wipe the whole of the earth out. I have never tasted the tobacco in her mouth. At least not in this version. And I have no memory of the many times I might have tasted the tobacco in her mouth, many versions ago.

Neva drops her bags and runs towards the toilet. Ana says something but I can't understand what she says.

Grey Tropic

Once again, I don't think they are speaking English.

§

Ten minutes or so later, after resisting heroically for a while but surrendering in the end, I'm chopping onions in the kitchen. The windows are all steamed up, the water is boiling in a pan. Slices of tomato, cubic, the size of a normal dice, lay in wait for the moment they'll be turned into a cheap, simple, but tasty sauce to go with the fusilli. *Fusilli.* The ease with which I can think the word fusilli makes me wonder whether I'm Italian. Am I Italian? Why am I in charge of cooking this pasta? Why was I volunteered by Neva? What does she know that I don't?

I can hear them laughing in the kitchen. The three of them — stoned again and laughing. I resent them. Why, I don't know. But I suspect that they are laughing about my dream, about the disappointment I've been through after realising I had been fooled for almost 2 whole parts of this novella. Novella — it would appear I have now come to accept this classification. Every now and then I hear them speak in hissy whispers. They laugh in whispers, too, the sound of the air leaving their bodies, their snorts, betraying their laughter from the other room — happy people are the bane of existence, particularly for those chopping onions. I balance for a moment whether I should just get the pan of boiling water and run at them and burn them to death and batter the shit out of their twitching charred bodies with the pan until they are cold and resembling mash left overnight on a plate. I don't do it.

I spit in the boiling water instead — that's what an Italian would do. And now I feel much better.

§

Ten minutes or so later we're eating the pasta. They are eating the pasta, completely oblivious to my anger and resentment. They eat the pasta, they eat my gob, they eat in silence, enjoying every bite, commenting every now and then with a sybarite *hmmm*. I can only hope they don't read this draft. It would be unpleasant to have them confront me about the spitting in some other rewrite. I finish my food. Rescue a joint from the depths of the ashtray. Smoke looking at the rain hit the window, while they finish the rest of their food in silence. The rain falls in tears, getting lost behind the plants in the window frame. I have déjà vu. Then more déjà vu. *Poi ho un altro déjà vu.*

§

Grey Tropic

Ten minutes or so later they have finished eating and we're all smoking together, another spliff that Neva has rolled, and it tastes like her spit tasted in the kissing scene that never made it to the final draft. My resentment has vanished. So has — after just a couple of minutes — my guilt for spitting in their food. Everything passes, everything does; this too shall pass, even this rather unnecessary diversion. Spitting can also be a nice gesture. The exchange of saliva can be something good. We could think that the spit has been my way of kissing the three of them. This has been well reported by Orientalist anthropologists, about innumerable cultures.

Neva, Ana and Henry pass the joint around. They smoke — pleasure tickles their faces. They have praised my food. They have praised the company. They have even praised the weather, the monstrous and insane weather that has kept us together, in this tiny room in Rue St Maur — they have implied the weather has brought us together: it makes no sense. Now they are praising Paris, flooding Paris. Soon they'll end up praising the values of the Enlightenment. This could end up in something very reactionary, somewhere properly right-wing libertarian. But I will miss all this part, because my brain will take me elsewhere. To films in French.

Fernando Sdrigotti & Martin Dean

The first image I will tell you about is of Marlon Brando, shouting "fucking God!" in the opening scene of a misogynistic flick about rape with saxophone music. Then Jean-Pierre Léaud trashing Maria Schneider around at Bir Hakeim metro station, same film — there's something uncannily aesthetic about this scene of domestic albeit public violence. Then Audrey Tatou buying fruit from a French-Algerian greengrocer, in a film about a French colour blind *ingenue* who doesn't enjoy sex very much and has a thing for garden gnomes. And then, Jean-Paul Belmondo walking down St Germain with a junky selling copies of the *Washington Post* — but this one almost sepia, fading, not very clearly anchored in my brain; I don't even know why this one comes to me, for it isn't a very good film at all. Not like Jean-Pierre Léaud, once more, drinking coffee at Les Deux Maggots with a blonde, after stalking her, in a film about him being a bit of a tosser and two women who love him in different ways, a very moody thing trying to portray the atmosphere of the storm of nihilist shit that was unleashed after May 68. And Delphine Seyrig, the mother of all sexy mature ladies in your area dying to meet you, sneaking in the room of a post-adolescent, once more played by Jean-Pierre Léaud — furtive and smelly sex in a Parisian afternoon, Delphine relieving

Jean-Pierre of his blue balls, in that cloudy afternoon some fifty years ago. And then Jean-Pierre Léaud, running away from something or someone, as a kid, the pigeons fly into the air, scared by Jean-Pierre Léaud as a kid. And Jean-Pierre Léaud playing a record in an automated record booth. Jean-Pierre Léaud. Jean-Pierre Léaud. Always Jean-Pierre Léaud, the visible face of pretentious French cinema. Jean-Pierre Léaud, the visible face of moody, taciturn and chain-smoking French baby boomers. Everything has become about Jean-Pierre Léaud, that's the way things are right here right now. Why, I don't have a clue. A terrible idea takes me by assault. I run to the toilet and wash my face. I'm tormented by the idea of Jean-Pierre Léaud — Jean-Pierre Léaud, his existence, his immaculate hair, even in old age. Jean-Pierre Léaud. The sound of the name, which I can't pronounce, torments me. Is it Leóu? Is it Leáu? I wash myself, let the water run for a bit on the back of my head. When I raise my eyes and spot my own face in the mirror I confirm what I suspected: I'm Jean-Pierre Léaud. Jean-Pierre Léaud. Jean-Pierre Léaud. Jean-Pierre Léaud, I repeat, several times, each time a bit better, each time sounding more and more like Jean-Pierre Léaud.

Of course I would! Of course. I mean, I'm not Jean-Pierre Léaud himself. But I'm made in his resemblance.

I had never been described this far in this story — this should have raised suspicions. But didn't anyone else notice this? Did the reader notice this?

I walk fast into the front room and catch Neva wrapping up a sentence that ends in "as Bastian says, these have all been hijacked by the immaculately dressed poets of the everyday." I have no idea of what she's talking about — Ana and Henry have no idea either, their faces betray they have stopped listening ages ago. I stand there, at the threshold between toilet and kitchen and lounge, paralysed. The paralysis in my face, my body language must catch their attention.

"WHAT'S WRONG?" asks Neva without even stopping after "everyday".

"I'm Jean-Pierre Léaud!" I shout.

"Yes!" says Ana, carefree. Henry nods. They go back to talk to each other, in some language I can't understand. They welcome my interruption, the exit plan I grant them for free.

"And…" says Neva, moving her right hand for me to continue, in a rather patronising way.

"Is that not enough? I'm Jean-Pierre Léaud!" The three of them stare at me blankly. Neva looks at me with a serious face. She takes her right hand to her fake reading glasses.

"Didn't you know?" she asks with a pedagogical

tone.

"NO!"

The first one to laugh is Ana. Henry follows. Neva tries to hold the laughter for a while and then starts laughing too. I'm mad at them. Mad at the world. Mad at this story. Mad like only Jean-Pierre Léaud could be. And suddenly I'm no longer mad and I'm laughing too. I laugh and tears flood my eyes. Suddenly it doesn't feel so bad to be Jean-Pierre Léaud, although I don't remember Léaud laughing in any film.

"I can't believe you didn't know!" says Neva. "You must have forgotten. Or it could be a narrative inconsistency. Haven't you looked at your face in a mirror, a window, a bottle?"

"Not that I recall. No."

"That's not true," says Henry. There was a moment in part one when you threw up — you might have looked at your face in the mirror. You can't throw up without looking at your face in the mirror afterwards. It's one of the rules: you puke you look."

"This is not a film, Henry!" I say.

"He's right," says Ana. "*Askantifara rulhuye veidicamenteo*," she says to Henry. Henry nods.

"I can't believe no one told me!" I shout.

"Take it easy, Capricorn," says Neva.

"It's easy to say! I wish I had known. This whole

thing would have been different."

"How so?" asks Neva.

"I would have known I was Jean-Pierre Léaud. It would have felt different. Perhaps things would have had a reason to be."

"A *raison d'etre*," says Ana.

"*Oui*," I say, now fully aware that I'm Jean-Pierre Léaud and perhaps fluent in French — this is needless to say a bit disconcerting because I don't speak French.

"Let's go for a walk," says Neva, perhaps realising I'm truly confused.

"OK," I say, without questioning the lack of coherence of her invitation — after all it is raining. And after all, this story is deeply incoherent too. Out it will be; out in the rain. For some reason.

We put our shoes on in silence, walk down the stairs in silence, grab two umbrellas from the bucket downstairs, any two umbrellas, in silence — Neva gets Galleries Lafayette and I get Yves Saint Laurent. We leave the building in Rue St Maur in silence, open our umbrellas in silence, and start walking down the road in silence, Neva in front while I follow behind.

She's incredibly bow-legged and I love her. Even if I never kissed here. Even if I never had a complicated moment of sentimental ennui about her, as Jean-Pierre Léaud would have had, perhaps for no reason at all. Do

Grey Tropic

I love her? What is love? Is love possible? Is love just confusion by other means? I need a cigarette. I need a cigarette and a coffee. I rearrange my hair in wind. My hair is long and dark, too long for a man, too dark for my age. My hair is dyed and coiffed. My hair is amazing.

VUE PRISE DE LA TOUR DE L'HORLOGE DE LA GARE DE LYON - 29 JANVIER 1910

5.

A black boot steps on a used condom on Avenue de la République. The owner of the boot never realises he has stepped on a used condom and keeps on walking. The man and the woman walking behind him keep on moving in the direction of Père Lachaise. As they disappear into the distance the condom twitches on the floor, almost as if it were alive. The spunk inside moves from one fold to the other — for it is a textured condom, dark brown in colour. Some of the air bubbles inside it burst. New bubbles appear.

The sidewalk is, all the sidewalks are, cluttered with all sort of rubbish carried with the water. Condoms, yes, but also cigarette butts, leaves, organic substances impossible to tell without proper lab analysis, lost lighters, broken umbrellas, copper € coins, a couple of letters addressed to a Madame Mariam Antoun, domiciled in Rue Spinoza, some number in Rue Spinoza no longer visible, fragments of pages in French, from newspapers, magazines, now impossible to read, their letters blending into an orgy of fonts, a cacophony of words were _e Pen and _aris and __rka and _acron can still be guessed.

From the viewpoint of the condom, almost too far to be properly seen, behind a crumbled packet of Gitanes (obviously) that half-blocks the view — from the viewpoint of the condom, of course — can be seen Neva and Ariel reaching

Grey Tropic

the corner where Avenue de la République, Boulevard de Ménilmontant, and Avenue Gambetta meet.

§

We walk under the rain; we've been walking for a while now. We're the only people here but at least it isn't that muddy. Every now and then Neva breaks the silence and points towards this or that tomb — ineluctably the dead will be a celebrity. Mainly literary celebrities but celebrities nevertheless. Maybe not in this order but we walk past Proust, Wilde (a tomb that looks like an Assyrian angel, covered in glass, the monument behind the glass covered in kisses), Molière, Balzac, some other names I forget because I don't register them — this is not the kind of thing my memory bothers to register. But beyond my memory or lack of it, this feels like walking through the library of a literary snob or a critic, or a literature professor; it's pointless but somehow interesting in an anecdotical way. And we get music too. Chopin, Piaf, and Neva says also Jim Morrison. I ask to be taken to see Morrison's grave, of all the dead celebrities, I don't know why. Neva asks if I like The Doors. I say I don't but that I'm curious nevertheless, trying to second guess my own intentions. Why, she asks. Because, I say. She tuts and turns around and walks in silence, once again. She stops pointing here or there because she's mad at me. Or perhaps here and there there isn't anybody worthy of being mentioned. Our silences must mean something. But I can't figure out what this might be. At some point I got lost and I still am. And that's the only thing that matters now.

We walk for what must be ten minutes, taking turns that seem to me whimsical — it feels as if we were going in circles, or at least as if Neva didn't know where we're heading to. We walk past a wall, at least three times. There's a sign with golden letters and flowers lying at its feet. Neva is lost. She has to be lost. There's no way she can't not be lost.

"Remind me about that," says Neva, pointing at the wall, the third time we walk past it. "I'll tell you about it when we stop to have a cup of coffee, or to eat, or to have a whisky, whatever it is you people do."

"What is it?"

"I'll tell you when we stop to have a cup of coffee, or to eat, or to have a whisky, whatever it is you people do."

"You've said that already."

"Exactly." Yes, she is moody.

We walk a bit longer and then Neva's body language changes — she seems looser, relaxed and confident, all at once, her shoulders even relax, loosen, drop: she has found her bearings, she has recovered some form of agency over the spatial design of the cemetery, over the urbanists who decided to come up with this city of the dead, perhaps expecting people to get lost in it, a fitting metaphor for life and death, and for the city of the not yet dead around it. We walk towards another corner of the cemetery and two or three minutes later we're standing two or three metres away from a tombstone, rectangular, not impressive in size nor design. There's an Asian girl sitting on it, under her bright white L'Oreal umbrella, holding a piece of paper in her right hand (a photograph), a bunch of flowers on her left, her eyes flooded with tears, her hair and make up slightly messed up, righty messed up, messed up in the right way — she's broken and beautiful. We give her room to perform her ritual.

"She seems touched," says Neva, as she moves closer to me.

"Touched like in groped?" I ask.

"No, fool! Touched as emotionally overcome by the aura of Jim Morrison's tomb."

"Oh... But I can't see no aura, Neva. I thought the tomb was different... Are you sure this is the same Jim Morrison I was asking about? The guy who used to wear leather trousers and sing songs about fucking his mother?"

"I'm positive it's the same Jim Morrison," says Neva, still holding my arm, staring at me, the two of us under our umbrellas, under the rain.

"I thought it was a different tomb. I thought there was a bust of Morrison. Something covered in graffiti and love messages. I remember seeing it in some magazine, back in the early 90s or so… When it was the 20th anniversary of his death."

"God, you are old!" says Neva and shakes me by my elbow and the drops falling from my umbrella fall faster.

"Yes, I am," I say. "I'm on my way out. The climax has been reached and I'm now descending."

"I don't think this had been addressed before," says Neva. "I mean, your *old* age, in the text, of course… This hasn't been addressed before."

"This is full of gaps, dear," I say.

"I find that expression incredibly sexy," says Neva and she looks at me wanting to be kissed. I should kiss her, I really should. But just as I am about to kiss her we hear the girl by the tomb sobbing, quite loud, and then wailing. And now she's holding her head in her hands, crying her eyes out, holding the picture against her chest. Suddenly she stands up, throws the umbrella to the side, leaves the photograph and the flowers on the tomb, and runs away holding her face.

Grey Tropic

"That was very dramatic," I say.

"Yes, it was," says Neva. "It was like a moment of reckoning, whatever that means."

"I'm not sure you mean that but I know where you're coming from," I say.

We move closer to the tombstone now. It's a sober tombstone, and this somehow contradicts the fact that this is Jim Morrison's tomb. The Lizard King. The pop star who wanted to be a writer or a poet and who used to drink beer in the morning. Beer and fag, break on through blah blah blah. Hitchhiking and killing drivers, burying them in the desert. Ghost songs. Fast cars, LA women, and cultural appropriation. The photograph is facing down, the flowers are lying like flowers lie, the umbrella is also lying, on the floor, its handle pointing to the sky in a 45 degrees angle, slowly filling with water. I move closer to the picture, grab it, turn it around. It's the famous photograph of Jim posing with his arms spread, his hairy chest surrendered to the photographer, to the lustful camera-eye, to the camera-lover — a camera that betrays desire. Jim is there, his arms open, waiting to catch flight, waiting to smash the world, cross the dark divide, towards eternity. Jim, good old Jim, square-jawed Jim. Pure American flesh and bone. His curls, his beautiful eyes. Jim who died at 27, who started the myth of the 27 club (or was it Janis or was it Jimi or was it James? It was James, Deano, James Dean; it had to be an American man; it had to be a Jimbo). But here good old Jim Morrison, lying below my feet, feeding maggots since 1971, now looking at me, looking at me from those familiar yet uncannily alien eyes. Looking at me from those eyes I know and fail to know, that I don't know anymore. Looking at me, wanting to do things to my soul kitchen, Jim, good old Jim, tampering with the gay in me. Yes, I used to like The Doors. Yes, I used to love The Doors. Yes, I had a massive crush on Jim. Yes. It must have been ages ago. It must have been centuries ago. It must have been, it was, my childhood, the soundtrack to my first joints, my firsts pills, my first quarter of LSD, being chased down the road by equestrian statues, having awful sex with girls and boys with Ramones t-shirts, cumming in my pants at the wrong moment. It must have been another life, for — in the same way I can't recognise myself — I can't recognise Jim any more. I can't say "hey, Jim, rest in peace, man, I used to love you, dude, man, partner, lover." I have forgotten his face. And even worse: I have forgotten the words that would allow me to talk to him, that would allow me to tell him how much I think I need him, how much I miss him, how much I miss those years, now that I'm on the long — hopefully long — way out. We're

Grey Tropic

strangers now, Jim and I. Strangers like my current self and who I used to be some years ago.

"That's not Jim Morrison," says Neva, interrupting my thoughts.

"I have forgotten him, too," I say. "I was pondering over that. Time's a bitch."

"What?"

"Yes. I was thinking that I couldn't recognise Jim Morrison's face any more... I concede — I used to love The Doors. I used to love Jim: I used to love Ray Marzarek's stupid keyboard. Even that!"

"That's Val Kilmer," says Neva.

"What do you mean?"

"That's not Jim Morrison — that's a film still. That's Val Kilmer."

I look at the picture better — yes, it's Val Kilmer. Val Kilmer as Jim Morrison. Val Kilmer before bloating like Jim towards the end. Val Kilmer, the guy from *Top Secret* and *Top Gun* and *Batman*. Val, another chisel-jawed American with a name that sounds onomatopoeic. Another good looking mancrush. Another hellraiser. But not Jim Morrison. I can't love Val — my heart belongs to Jim.

"You are right!" I say. "Is Val Kilmer buried here?"

"To the best of my knowledge he's alive," says Neva. "We all look the same to Asians, I guess," she says.

The potentially problematic observation fills me with sadness. We should probably be laughing but we're sad. We're both filled with sadness, I believe. I don't even know why. Oliver Stone's film was bad but it really wasn't that bad. Perhaps it's the realisation of how disposable we are.

We place Val Kilmer's photo on Jim Morrison's tomb, by the flowers, both sheltered from the rain with the L'Oreal umbrella, its handle hanging loosely, inviting the wind to take it on a upwards Mary Poppins kind of journey.

And we leave the cemetery.

§

Neva lights up and blows the smoke into the air. I grab one of her cigarettes and light up too and I blow the smoke into the air too, but through my nose. It feels contrived, forced, and I can't remember whether I smoked before during this story or not but this moment requires a cigarette. Of course everyone else is smoking around us — I wonder what the cancer stats are like over here.

We're sitting in the terrace area in a café across the road from the cemetery. If it rained from the west we would be soaked. But it rains from the south and so far the canopy is enough of a cover to keep ourselves and other ten or so other punters safe from the water. Neva smokes in silence, staring forward, towards the entrance to the metro station or the cemetery wall, this is not clear. I mean, I could ask her what she's staring at, but it wouldn't add anything, would it? She's just smoking, letting the smoke out with sighs, staring at the metro entrance or the cemetery wall. That's all that matters.

There's something about this staring that should tell me something, there must be a reason why this slightly ignorant narrator I'm playing right here stops at these details — what do I want to say? I should be concentrating on that right now instead on whether she's staring here or there. The staring wants to tell me something. If only I could realise that she wants to tell me something like this, through her taciturn — perhaps moody — staring; if I could figure that out I could communicate it. If only the narrator part of myself and myself as a character weren't disassociated. Or if only I were an omniscient narrator and not just a poor observer of the world around me. But I am disassociated and not omniscient at all. And so I also smoke looking at the escalator to the left of where we are, completely ignorant of Neva's mood, her needs, whatever this might be — I'm such a man — so unaware.

My mind is locked on the escalator now: it's like a production line of people. They all come out with their umbrellas already open. It's like a moving advertisement hoarding — there's something beautiful about it. Activia. Christian Dior. Cartier. BNP Paribas. Veuve Clicquot. Renault. Societé Générale. Givenchy. EDF. Novotel. Lafarge. Michelin. Rémy Martin. Alliance and Leicester. Kérastase. Veolia — which sounds in my mind almost like I imagine *voilà* to sound — is this intentional? Alliance and Leicester? I spot this umbrella again. The ginger guy covering his head with it. He crosses the road and comes towards us. He's wearing an Alliance and Leicester t-shirt and Alliance and Leicester shorts. I elbow Neva and point at the guy.

"What's with him?" asks Neva.

"I think I know him. But I can't remember where from…" I say.

"Paris isn't a big city. You might have bumped into him earlier. He likes Alliance and Leicester, that's for sure," says Neva and goes back to her staring, trying to make a point of some kind. Once again I fail to understand which point she's trying to make while the Alliance and Leicester guy disappears around the corner and I stay with him in my mind — he feels like another *dèjá vu*. There must be a reason why I'm stopping my train of thought to think about him. There must be a reason why he's here. Or not; maybe not. Because soon I forget about him and go back to watching more people leaving the escalator for a while. Rhodia. Orange. Hachette. Ubisoft. Bolloré. Hermès. Gaumont. Crédit Agricole. Pentalog. Sodexo. Saint-Gobain. Yoplait. Citroën. Decathlon. Bouygues. Pathé. It goes on and on and on. It could go on all day.

Neva finishes her cigarette and crushes it with her right foot. She looks at me from behind two deep expression marks on her forehead, trenches of anger or disappointment.

"Well…"

"Well what?"

"Well… If you don't want to know, fuck it, I won't tell you!"

"What are you talking about?"

"You were supposed to remind me of something, weren't you?"

"Oh, shit, right! The wall! Sorry, I forgot."

"The wall! Fuck the wall now! You are clearly not interested in the wall. Fuck the wall! Otherwise you would have reminded me, if you had wanted to know about the wall. But alas it's my fault, no one should be forced to want to know! You're right — I'm a fool."

She lights another cigarette and goes back to watching her spot somewhere towards the front right.

"I'm sorry — it's not like that… Look, I want to know! Really. I'm curious."

"If you really wanted to know you wouldn't have forgotten to remind me… That's the way things are. I'm a grown-up — I can live with it," she says without looking at me.

"I have other things on my mind. I apologise," I say. "Do tell me, please. I want to know. I really want to know what's with that wall."

"Do you mean it?" she says, looking in my direction — she's less angry now.

"I never meant anything more than this, Neva," I say. I really believe I never meant anything more than this. Her eyes betray that she realises that I truly believe it. Her eyes are full of light now.

"That's the Communards Wall," she says and raises her eyebrows.

"Really?"

"Yes!" she says.

"Wow! And what's that?" I ask.

"You don't have a clue, do you?"

"No, not at all. Tell me everything!" She stares at me examining me. Do I really mean it? I really don't but I don't want to summon her ire. So I do my best to feign interest, raising my eyebrows and opening my eyes, like her, believing once more that I want to know, that I care, that I am — indeed — interested.

"Sure?"

"Yes! Go on!"

"Well... I'm writing about this right now, I did tell you something already... A historical novel... It's a very interesting story — quite fascinating. The wall, that's the spot where around one hundred fifty communards were shot in 1871... That precise spot. Think about that. One hundred fifty communards shot, and buried, not far from there. And we just walked past all that. And I walk past there almost every day — it's like stepping over history, over the dead of history, a line that could circle the earth several times, and yet a reaffirmation of life, in some way. Just one hundred fifty of those murdered by history in this city. Think about that."

"Well, it's a cemetery..."

"You know what I mean, fool!"

"Yes, I do." I don't.

"The story of the communards is really fascinating," she says, now fully in communard mood, when the only communards I can think of are Jimmy Sommervile and Richard Cole. "That's the spot. They were shot there and then buried in a mass grave in

Père Lachaise." Images of Sommervile and Cole being executed by who knows who come to my mind. "It's an important spot. A spot that perhaps explains the doomed path the Twentieth century would take. Perhaps even the path this one is taking, all things considered," says Neva. Think about that: that wall, that wall, that wall might explain it all."

"I bet it does."

"But it get more interesting," she says.

"Can it?" I say.

"It is widely believed..." she says and stops, looking for the right words. "It is widely believed, wrongly believed, by many that is, that the spot where they were shot is elsewhere. Many people think that the actual spot is outside, on an outer wall, at the site of Paul Moreau-Vauthier's monument to the Victims of the Revolution. But Moreau-Vauthier's monument actually commemorates the victims of this period, regardless of who they were killed by. It's an attempt at a pathetic Theory of the Two Demons, if you know what I mean: everyone was equally evil; all political violence is equally wrong, blah blah blah. This is a fucking reactionary lie! And people still get these monuments wrong!"

"I see. That's remarkable," I say.

"It is, isn't it? Such a gross mistake. And it doesn't

end there. There was even a two hundred Zlotych banknote — that's Polish money by the way — that celebrated the life and you could even say the heroic death of one of the Polish communards, who was executed in Père Lachaise with his French comrades. The banknote used the image of Moreau-Vauthier's monument. A gross mistake, if we consider the fact that Moreau-Vauthier was a pig!"

"That's even more remarkable," I say and grab Neva's cigarettes and light one to keep my mouth busy for a while. I guess Neva is a journalist but also an academic of some sort. Which might explain her slightly disheveled and graceless physical appearance and why she knows Henry, who isn't an academic and could never be one but likes to surround himself with people with degrees and titles, just to compensate for his abject ignorance and intellectual weakness. I'm of course puzzled by this: I never clocked any trace of academia in her — I never saw it coming, not until this conversation, this conversation that could be full of footnotes, actual footnotes on the page. I can't say I don't feel betrayed — I feel betrayed, in some way, and I don't even know why. Why didn't she break it to me? Why didn't she tell me that when she was introduced to me as a writer and journalist what was meant was that she's a PhD candidate. Candidate, what a spiteful word.

"Are you doing a PhD on this topic, by any chance?" I ask.

"Are you mad?" she asks — she seems offended.

"Sorry. I didn't mean like an insult, you now. There's nothing wrong with being a PhD candidate."

"What made you think I could be a PhD candidate? Candidate, what a horrible world," she says, repeating word for word — more or less — what I've just thought.

"I don't know… Henry… This conversation… Why would you befriend Henry unless you were an academic? He seems to want to surround himself with academic types. He gets an aura of intelligence from being around people who research and write about pointless stuff no one really cares about. He loves them. He gets kudos and a reputation from them. I don't know what they get in return. And why would you be interested in this communard thing unless you were bumping your CV writing papers about it? I know: I'm full of prejudice."

"No. No. You're right… In some way. It's an interest that is difficult to justify, particularly from a narrative point of view, in this story. But you're also wrong in another way: you are Henry's friend — you are having this conversation as well. By your same logic I should be wondering if you are an academic or not. But I'm not. And do you want to know why?"

"Yes, I do want to know why," I say, "although I suspect you have read a synopsis of this story, or something like that — something where the bottom of the iceberg that is my biography is fully explained, if you know what I mean."

"No, it's not that. That's not why I don't suspect you of anything."

"And why then?"

"Because I'm in love with you, I think," she says.

"Really?"

"No, I'm joking," she says. "Let's go."

"Where to?"

"You'll see."

She gets up and starts walking towards the metro. We forget to pay and a waiter covering himself with a Cinémathèque Française umbrella comes rushing after us. I pay. He tells me to go fuck my mother, in some Slav language I can't understand. But he definitely tells me to go fuck my mother. It must be Morrison's influence.

§

It smells musty and wet, aside from the usual smell of

armpits and dirty hair to be found in any packed train. The rattling and movement gives me an erection, that I believe is unrelated to the musty and wet smell and the armpits and dirty hair. It's a nice erection, albeit one uncalled for. I wonder whether I should rub myself against Neva, who's standing before me, against the seats, but I decide this would make the story take a dark and rapey turn. And this is not the way things should go, in my honest opinion — the tide has turned and with the exception of Houellebecq, Amis (Jr), some minor writers from the Global South (culturally relativised, their chauvinism tolerated) and a handful of older guys, no one is allowed gratuitous misogyny in their stories any more. Not saying that this is my story, though. But I'm glad I won't be rubbing myself against Neva.

"We get off at the next one," she says.

"Cool."

The next one is Bir-Hakeim, where many others also get off. The fresh air, the lack of rattling, send my cock back to sleep — I welcome this change, this move away from potentially dangerous territories. I follow Neva to the escalator, bow-legged Neva, the skinny and brittle Neva, the amateur historian (but not a nazi), the writer, her shoulders hunching, her bony back moving out of sync with the rest of her body, like a faulty toy, so graceless Neva. I follow her out and when we leave the station we continue walking straight. There's no need to open our umbrellas because we start to walk protected by a long bridge, on which trains cross the Seine from one side to the other. Everybody had the same idea — it feels like Oxford Circus on a Saturday afternoon, all the passersby sheltering from the rain under the narrow and long bridge, carrying their colourful umbrellas under their arms. Two lines have formed, perhaps naturally: we are on the right, walking north; the people on the left walk south. We all move more or less at the same speed; we all move orderly and without speaking, without flinching, without doubt, or fear — a long human line advancing towards the future or at least towards the other side of the river. Suddenly Neva pats me on the left elbow and points towards the right. The Eiffel Tower. I hadn't seen it before in this trip, not while awake. I think for a while the turn in the story that could have found us escaping this planet with the Eiffel Tower and chuckle.

"What?" asks Neva.

"Nothing. I remembered something incredibly stupid."

"Care to share it?"

"Oh, it's nothing," I say.

"Come on!"

"When I was a child I thought the Eiffel Tower was an interplanetary rocket," I say. I don't know why I lie.

"That's kind of cute," she says.

"It's stupid."

"You're strange, Capricorn," she says.

We keep walking under the bridge. Soon we reach the other bank and then a road. People disperse right and left. There's an elevated footpath ahead and we continue down the footpath and so do others. Until Neva stops abruptly — somehow no one bumps into her. Then she continues towards the left, missing people by millimetres, and leans against the railings. I move close to her — I miss everyone too, almost as if everyone else was a figment of someone's imagination or as if our movements were choreographed. Passersby — imagined or real — continue walking to my sides. No one tuts or huffs.

"Look," she says and points to the building just before us. It's a typical Parisian building, all the way from the bottom to its attic in what would be the sixth floor. It's a nice building. But there's nothing remarkable about it.

"Nice building," I say.

"Do you know it?"

"Nope."

"A film was shot here."

Grey Tropic

"Was it?"

"And it involves you."

"Me?

"Well, Jean-Pierre Léaud…"

I had forgotten about it. The reminder doesn't feel unpleasant. It's just a reminder, a nudge — I'm Jean-Pierre Léaud's doppelgänger, so be it. I arrange my dark and long hair, too dark and too long for a man my age. I crave tobacco. I crave something acerbic to say. I can't think of anything. I'm a pound shop Jean-Pierre Léaud.

"I don't know which film," I say.

"You're not even trying," says Neva.

"That's true. I'll try. Help me…"

"Look around. You were going on about it — in one of your mental monologues — a while ago."

"I won't ask you how you know about the monologues — the draft, yes… But how much do you know about…"

"Do you mean if I know about the boner in the train?" I don't reply. "You should have tried it. Who knows what would have happened…"

"Who knows…"

"Exactly, who knows… Now: WHAT FILM?"

"I don't know, you tell me!"

"*Last Tango in Paris!*"

"You are right!" I turn around and look back at the bridge. Yes that was the place where Brando fucking god'ed. And this is the bridge where Maria Schneider walks into the film, jumping over the rubbish collected by a street sweeper, and into a season of buggery and abuse. "Do you like the film?"

"I hate it," says Neva.

"And why bring me here then?"

"I thought it might stimulate an otherwise non-existent sexual impulse in you," she says. "Even if it's an impulse of the tormented kind. Even if this has to be done by tampering with your problematic masculine infantile mind. And even if it means talking about that horrible film. It had to be done."

"Meaning?"

"Meaning this is the part when you stop being a wuss and you take me to your hotel and we fuck."

"Do you mean that? Do you really think we should fuck? Do you find Jean-Pierre Léaud attractive?"

She pulls me from the collar of the shirt and kisses me. Her kiss tastes like tobacco and coffee. Is this another dream sequence? No, it isn't. This is real fiction.

"This isn't a dream sequence," she says, once more reading my mind. Then she kisses me once more. She pulls my body against hers and there isn't that much flesh to feel, just her warmth and her saliva and her breathing.

We stop kissing.

"Let's go," she says and then we rush to Passy Metro station, get on a train to Charles de Gaulle Étoile, and then change and get another train to Pigalle, and then change and get another train to Lamarck Caulaincourt. We hardly speak. The time passes quite quickly.

Five or six lines or so later we are leaving our umbrellas in the hotel's foyer and I'm sneaking her into my room. It feels like a crime. A beautiful crime.

§

"I'm a hungry kitten," says Neva taking a short break from sucking my dick. And then she goes back to it.

"I'm about to cum!" I announce but she keeps blowing and I shoot inside her mouth. She makes strange noises with her nose, struggles a bit trying to swallow pages of spunk and then gives up and runs to the toilet and spits in the basin.

"Jesus Christ, Capricorn, you almost choked me there!" she shouts from the toilet.

"Well, I did warn you!"

"You didn't say you'd cum that much!" she says. I can then hear her gargling.

"Sorry!"

She comes back, still naked and lies next to me. She kisses me and I can feel the taste of my own cum in her mouth — there's something bleachy about it, the taste of the smell of bleach, the taste of the smell of Jean-Pierre Léaud's cum — cinematic cum, nihilist post 68 molotov-nostalgic cum, very masculine and complex cum. She turns around and grabs her cigarettes from the night table, lights up and passes the packet my way. I light up and we both smoke staring at the roof. If this were a film and there was music in this scene, the music would be "Les amants de Paris", like in *La maman et la putain*, in that scene where the beautiful Bernadette Lafont smokes a whole cigarette, leaning against a wall, while Piaff sings from a vinyl player. But was she smoking? It doesn't matter. What matters is that I believe she came too — Neva, not Bernadette — but I can't be sure and I'm willing to take the blame for not knowing.

"Right," she says. "That's done."

"What's done?"

"I can tick that off my bucket list. 'Fuck Capricorn': ticked."

"Well, at least it was about Capricorn and not Jean-Pierre Léaud."

"Both," she says. "I can now tick both."

She gets up from the bed, still smoking, moves closer to the window and opens the curtains, just a bit. I watch her, with her back to me, her back and arse and legs surrendering their malnourished beauty to me, with unaware confidence.

"Where's the dick twanger's room? No, I didn't read it in a draft — Henry told me about it."

"It's the one across the garden, a floor down."

She moves closer to the window. Looks down.

"I can't see any window on the floor below this one," says Neva. I jump from my bed and move close to her; I toss the cigarette into the garden and then shut the window, open the curtains fully. When I look to the place where Stephan's dick would be, there's nothing. I mean, not nothing, not emptiness — there's a wall. I mean not on Stephan's body but blocking the view between us and the garden and his dick. If there is a dick being twanged on the other side it's impossible to tell: the place where the two windows were before, just a couple of days ago is now walled over. In all fairness it doesn't look like it has been walled over recently — it looks like it was always like that.

"I don't get it," I say, "I was pretty sure there was a window there."

"Well, there isn't one," says Neva. "And we haven't had sex still," she says and when she says that I realise she's with her clothes on.

"What's going on?" I ask and look at my own body — I'm wearing my clothes too.

"What are we doing in your room?" asks Neva and then the knocks on the door, audible, clear: *La cucaracha, la cucaracha, ya no puede caminar*. I motion for her to hide in the toilet. When she does I open the door: of course it's Stephan.

"Hi," he says and walks into the room. "She can come out," he says, pointing towards the toilet. "I won't tell — I don't need to say anything," he adds. Stephan is wearing a three-piece suit, light brown. He's wearing brogues and his moustache is waxed and pristine; he carries an umbrella under his right arm, a black umbrella, no logo visible. Neva comes out of the toilet. "Let me introduce myself," says Stephan, staring at Neva.

"Are you the dick twanger?" asks Neva and as she finishes asking this she lets a small cry out and a tooth, one of her front teeth, falls from her mouth and bounces on my right foot.

"Should I continue?" asks Stephan — he looks cross. Neva, with her right hand over her mouth, moves her head from one side to the other, several times. There are tears in her eyes. She's scared; I'm scared too; there must be tears in my eyes too. Our characters understand something that we can't fully grasp. But we must feel scared, that much we know.

"My name is Stephan and in this story I live across the garden, in one of the rooms on the lower floor... I also had a part in the dream sequence, and let's not dwell too much on that part... But I also happen to be a stand in for this piece's editor. Yes, that's right. Well, the editor, believes he — through me, considering the physical resemblance between us two — has been gratuitously misrepresented, as a creepy onanist. I regret that there won't be any of this. It's on the one hand libelous and also, potentially, if read in certain way, homophobic."

"I see," I say. "I understand your concerns... Or the editor's concerns," I add.

"There are valid concerns," says Stephan, assertive but calm, a world away from his previous fidgety and flustered self.

"Indeed... Let's say we remove this part from the story... Let's say the editor edits it out, without further action from our part, and with a solid promise that we will finalise the story in the best possible terms, and without further libel to you or the editor. Can we have our sex back? And her front tooth too, please."

"I'll see what can be done," he says and turns around.

"I'll do my best to forget what has happened, and to

influence the story as much as I can, from my humble role as the main character, that isn't much, but at least it's something... I will try my best," I say.

"I know you will," says Stephan. "Good evening," he says, nods at me and nods at Neva and closes the door behind him.

"Cum inside me!" says Neva, below me. I cum inside her and I fall over her naked body. My orgasm lasts for half a minute or so. When I pull out I stare at her beautiful labia open like a flower, wet, wetting the bed. I kiss her. I think I love her. And I completely forget about Stephan, until I read this story some years later. But when I read this story I'm no longer the main character and I'm going over the final draft.

§

A day passes. We have sex at least six more times. And then life goes on.

We leave the room and its intolerable stench of sexual fluids and go back to Neva's flat to pick up Ana and Henry. And then the four of us go out together. Ana and Henry got laid too. They don't need to tell us anything and I don't need to read any draft. There's an energy emanating from Henry that for the first time makes me feel like I don't want to punch him. Ana

Grey Tropic

looks happy too and she's not wearing her skates.

And now we are sitting under the arcades at the Place des Vosges. It's raining, of course it is; it might never stop. Paris has been flooding for weeks now. The Zouave has drowned under Pont del Alma. Square du Vert Galant has totally disappeared under the water. And soon it'll be the turn of the bridges, and then the water will overflow, inundate the wine cellars, possibly swallow the Louvre. A state of emergency has been declared and the army is already patrolling the lower areas of the city by boat. I don't care. I don't care if the city is sinking while we drink coffee. These moments are well beyond the weather, the climate, the circumstances around us. There's something eternal about what is going on right now, about us. It feels as if the four of us, yes, even Henry, post-coital-cool Henry, had been in this place, sitting at this table, in this exact bar, forever. Time has stopped. And we, bohemians, untainted by work, admin, mortgages, or responsibilities of any kind, here we are. We, writers without books, filmmakers without films, philosophers without concepts, painters without a painting, characters in books that haven't and will not be written, thank god. Thinkers without thoughts. People drinking coffee, just that.

And maybe this is our film; maybe we are in a film

and not in a book. Maybe we even are in someone's head. Maybe we are someone's thoughts. Whatever where we are: here we are. And that is the sole reason why we are beautiful. Beautifully Parisian. Even if only we are just passing by. And who's not passing by in this place? We are all passing. Surely no one belongs here. "*Sur le passage de quelques personnes à travers une assez courte unité de temps*," I say aloud, no longer surprised by my ability to speak French.

"Rats. Rats with wings," offers Neva and interrupts my mental monologue. She points toward six or seven pigeons pecking at a piece of wet bread, left in an ashtray, by an empty table. Their feet are submerged in the water; their feathers glued to their rickety bodies.

"I quite like them," says Ana.

"What?" says Henry, finally lifting his eyes from the menu.

"Yes. Those fucking pigeons. Rats with wings. They are horrible and they're making me sick."

"I thought you were talking about the kids," I say pointing at a group of kids kicking a ball around, sheltered from the rain under the arcades. Neva chuckles.

"Those are wingless pigeons," says Neva and she looks at me, and pulls her sun glasses down a little bit when she says it, and I feel Henry's eyes going from

Grey Tropic

her to me and me to her and then back into the menu.

Everything is a bit yellow. A sepia melancholia. We made love. Yes, that's the right way to put it. There's nothing to explain: Neva and I are in love. That is all there is. That is all there will ever be. There won't be any more departures. No goodbye kisses in Lamarck Caulaincourt — as in that very first draft that someone wrote in 2002, after that first visit to Paris. No Neva getting on a train, saying "*quelle merde*", looking at me from an empty train and me walking back to the hotel, getting my shoes off for no reason, leaving the shoes in a trash bin in Square Joël Le Tac, walking barefoot to the hotel and to room 29, going back to London wearing a pair of slippers. There won't be any of that. And especially no more trips back to London. No more living in the grey city across the Channel. No heavy drinking in dark pubs, next to stinky and taciturn people who never barge into your life for some small chat. No more waiting for death drinking beer, alone. None of that, I'll stay here. I'll live and die in Paris. With Neva.

If only I had a Super 8, or a 16mm, or a 35mm cinema camera. If only I could fix the beauty of this moment, our passage through this time, however flimsy and wanton. If only someone did, even someone else, even without our knowing. If only someone remembered all this. If only someone wrote it.

The wrinkles on Neva's eyes, and mine and Ana's slightly rotten teeth and Henry's strong body odour.

And the rain.

And the pigeons.

And those kids playing football under the arcade.

If only time could be fixed and this was all there ever was. For all eternity; for a never-ending number of pages. If only all this could be fixed. If only this could be fixed, serve as a shelter. From everything that is always lurking around the corner. A shelter. From all the shit that is always about to overflow. Like that brown river just a few blocks down the road.

FIN

ABOUT THE AUTHORS

Fernando Sdrigotti was born in Rosario (Argentina) in the late seventies. He is the author of *Dysfunctional Males*, *Shitstorm* and *Departure Lounge Music*, among other titles.

Martin Dean is a writer who lives in London.

Printed in Poland
by Amazon Fulfillment
Poland Sp. z o.o., Wrocław